The CHICKEN Doesn't SKATE

Other exciting books
by GORDON KORMAN:

Swindle

Zoobreak

Framed

Toilet Paper Tigers

Radio Fifth Grade

Dive trilogy

Everest trilogy

Kidnapped trilogy

Island trilogy

On the Run series

The CHICKEN Doesn't SKATE

GORDON KORMAN

SCHOLASTIC INC.
New York Toronto London Auckland
Sydney Mexico City New Delhi Hong Kong

ISBN 978-0-545-28925-2

12 11 10 9 8 7 6 5 4   12 13 14 15/0

Printed in the U.S.A.   40

This edition first printing, September 2010

For Michelle

The CHICKEN
Doesn't SKATE

1

RANGERS UPDATE:
CAPTAIN ADAM LURIE REPORTING

A science fair more important than hockey?

Give me a break! In this part of Minnesota, *nothing* is bigger than hockey. If the Moose People from Neptune invaded St. Martin during a big game, they'd encounter zero resistance. Everybody would be at the rink. Only the losers would be left to fight them off — a loser being anyone around here who doesn't skate.

Of course, I'm kind of biased since I'm pretty good at hockey. So good that I'm captain of the South Middle School Rangers, even though I'm only a seventh-grader. To be totally honest, I'm officially in sixth grade, but that's only because I flunked science last year. So I had to take it again in summer school and I kind of flunked that, too. In the summer, Rollerblade hockey is very big.

The bottom line is, I'm in all grade-seven classes except science, where I'm stuck with the little sixth-grade losers — a loser being anyone who can spend five seconds in that lab without going insane from boredom.

So my ears were receiving Mrs. Baggio raving about this year's science fair, but my mind was on the ice, stickhandling, stopping on a dime in a shower of snow, streaking down on a breakaway, he shoots, he —

"Does everybody have to enter the science fair?"

That was Zachary Gustafson. *Definite* loser. King of losers. Know why he was worried about doing a project? Because all that work might interfere with his writing schedule. Rumor has it the kid churns out dozens of screenplays and mails them off to these big-time film studios, who reject them because they stink. Not that I've read any, of course. I don't even want to think about such a boring thing in such a boring class. It's like boring squared!

"Naturally, everybody will be doing a project, Zachary," said the Bag. "But only one per grade will be entered in the fair."

Instantly, all eyes turned to Milo Neal. Milo is the reason why this dumb science fair is front page news in St. Martin. Check out the name: Milo *Neal*. His dad is Victor Neal, the famous astronomer. His TV show *The Universe and You* is the top-rated program on the Science Channel.

Victor Neal is sort of St. Martin's claim to fame. He

grew up right here. He and Milo's mom were high school sweethearts. The whole town followed his career. Man, when he won the Nobel Prize for charting all those galaxies, this place went apewire! We even threw him a parade. You'd have thought he'd won the Stanley Cup!

That parade had been Milo's first look at his parents' hometown. He must have been about nine. It was January — eighteen below — I've never seen anybody so cold in my life! I guess that's when it hit me. Professor and Mrs. Neal were native Minnesotans, but Milo had lived in Los Angeles all his life. To him, cold meant you had to wear socks. It must have been hard for him when, two years later, his folks got divorced and he and his mom left California and came back to St. Martin to live.

So that's why the son of the most famous scientist in the country was the center of attention in the lab that day. Not only was Milo expected to go to the science fair — he was expected to ace it.

"There are no restrictions," Mrs. Baggio went on, "except it has to be science —" she looked me straight in the eye — "which means it isn't going to be about hockey."

"What about ice?" I challenged. "That's pretty scientific."

"Very well, Adam, do ice," said the teacher. "But there had better not be any skates on it. Or pucks." She turned to the rest of the class. "Your topics must be approved by me by the end of the week."

Kelly Marie Ginsberg (loser) nudged my arm. "You're fixated on hockey."

Like that's a bad thing. "Yeah? So?"

"So a fixation could turn into an obsession," she insisted. "And that could turn into a psychosis."

I was going to give her another "Yeah? So?" but some of the gung-ho types started chiming in with their topics. Disgusted, I thought about my seventh-grade classes, where everybody played it cool.

"Bats," piped up Sheila Martel.

"Recycling," announced Kelly Marie.

"Dolphins."

"Solar energy."

A hush fell. Milo Neal had raised his hand.

"Yes, Milo?" The way the Bag almost whispered it, you'd have thought he was going to tell her where he hid the lost continent of Atlantis.

Milo pushed his Bertrand St. Rene glasses higher up on his nose. "My project will be entitled 'The Complete Life Cycle of a Link in the Food Chain.'"

Well, that must have been something good because Mrs. Baggio beamed like a lighthouse.

"That's so deep," breathed Kelly Marie. Ten to one she had no idea what he was talking about.

"Awesome!" added Zachary. Twenty to one for him.

I rolled my eyes. "Okay. I'll bite. What does it mean?"

The Bag was all over that. "Yes, Milo. What the class wants to know is the subject of your study. What link in the food chain?"

California Boy looked importantly around the classroom.

"The chicken."

2

DOWNLOADED FROM THE FILES
OF ZACHARY GUSTAFSON

TERROR IN THE SEWER

Scene 1

[INTERIOR SHOT: City sewer – night]

Dank, dirty, disgusting. Rats are everywhere. Out of the darkness come two figures running . . . MAX AND PAULINE, terrified.

PAULINE

(exhausted)

Oh, Max, I can't go on!

MAX

I think we've lost him!

> Suddenly, a giant mutant three-eyed ALLIGATOR rises
> up with a bloodcurdling roar. Rats scurry in fear.
>
> [CLOSE-UP: Rows of razor-sharp teeth, dripping with
> steaming toxic drool.]

PAULINE

Aaaaugh!

MAX

Aaaaugh!

> The mighty jaws come crushing down on —

"Whoaa!!"

All of a sudden, someone yanked the cafeteria bench right out from under me. My notebook flew one way, my pen the other, and I was lifted up by the waistband of my underwear.

"Wedgie!!" It was a chorus of voices behind me.

"Aw, come on —" I protested.

All at once, my assailants released me. *Crash!* I went down hard amid scattered laughter and applause.

My spinning head cleared just in time to catch a glimpse of Adam Lurie and a few other muscleheads from the hockey team sneaking out past the food line, trading high fives.

I'd show those guys. When I was the hottest screen-writer in Hollywood, I'd have my agent cut a deal with all the theaters in Minnesota not to let them get in to see any of my hit movies. Then I'd call the pay phone in front of the Rivoli on Main Street — from poolside at my Beverly Hills mansion. When Adam answered, I'd say, "How's thirty below, butt-brain?" He'd recognize my voice from my acceptance speech at the Academy Awards. That's when I'd said, "And a special *in your face!* to the South Middle School Rangers in St. Martin!"

I got to my feet, picked up my stuff, and set the bench up again. You can't let idiots interfere with your art. Now, where was I? Oh, yeah. The sewer . . .

PAULINE

Kill it! Kill it!

A giant slimy forked tongue shoots out of the ALLIGATOR's jaws and wraps around MAX's neck.

MAX

Let go of me, you repulsive reptile!

He struggles madly but is slurped down like a meat-ball. The ALLIGATOR celebrates with a mighty belch.

I stopped and chewed on my pen. No, that wasn't it. Who was Pauline going to marry in the final scene if I killed off Max? I scratched out the last part.

MAX

Let go of me, you repulsive reptile!

> As he struggles, MAX pulls out his Swiss Army knife
> and begins flipping utensils: the fork, the nail clippers,
> the toothpick, and . . . *a giant samurai sword!* He
> rears back and slices the ALLIGATOR's disgusting
> three-eyed head off. The eyes close, one at a time.

> MAX and PAULINE are doused by a fountain of green
> alligator blood.

ROLL OPENING CREDITS

What a great beginning: The audience gets to watch the alligator bleed to death in the sewer while their popcorn is still warm and buttery. *That's* entertainment! This could be my big break.

Of course, it takes more than just talent to make it in the movie business. You've got to have luck; you've got to have timing; and most of all you've got to have connections.

You could be the best writer in the world, but if nobody ever reads your screenplay, they can't turn it into a blockbuster movie. But if you know a director, or a producer, or someone who does — if your aunt's cat's former owner is a good friend of the third cousin of Steven Spielberg's bowling coach, you're in. You've got connections.

Unfortunately, it was tough to develop connections

when you were eleven years old and living two thousand miles and seventy Fahrenheit degrees away from Southern California —

Milo Neal walked into the cafeteria.

— unless the connections came to you! I'd been giving this a lot of thought. Milo's dad had connections coming out his ears! He was a big star on cable TV; his science books sold millions; and he was a famous rich guy living in L.A. He probably went to parties with all the actors and producers and directors. Victor Neal was the world's best connection! And he was right here under my nose!

Well, his son was, anyway. He lived in St. Martin with his mom. I know it looks bad — like I'd be friends with Milo just because of my career. But I actually liked Milo a lot — sort of. He was very serious, maybe even a little bit dull. Hard to get to know. To be totally honest, I only talked to the guy once and he ignored me. But we were going to be great friends. *I had to meet his father!*

And anyway, we had one thing in common. He was going to be a great scientist and I was going to be a great writer, so at least we were both going to be great. That part was definite.

"Hi, Milo. How's it going?"

Milo's eyebrows went up behind the Bertrand St. Rene glasses.

I refreshed his memory. "Zachary, from science class, remember?"

"Oh, yeah. Hi." He didn't know me. I could tell. That was because he never looked to the left or right in the lab. Weird guy, my best friend. He was probably very focused. Or he had a stiff neck.

So by this time I was panicking because there was no conversation. Suddenly something went "Peep!" and there was this little yellow head peering out of his tooled-leather knapsack.

I rolled up my notebook and brandished it like a weapon. "Hold still! There's a giant bug on your bag."

"That's not a bug," Milo said quickly. He reached back and brought out a small baby chick. "This is the beginning of my science project," he explained.

"Are you going to dissect it?" I asked, intrigued.

Milo looked down his long, straight nose at me. I've got to develop a look like this for when I move to California. It really makes the other guy feel like worm guts.

"I'm going to document the complete life cycle of this hatchling," Milo said finally. "As a link in the food chain, it feeds and grows until *it* becomes food."

"Far out," I said, not really paying attention. Who was I to try to understand the science project of Victor Neal's son? I reached out to pat the hatchling on its fuzzy head. Zap! The little beast pecked me! I sucked on my finger where it was bleeding. "If you need anybody to wring its little neck," I couldn't help but mutter, "I'm your man."

"Oh, no," said Milo, deadpan. "The proper way to slaughter a chicken is decapitation. But this one's not nearly old enough, of course."

What? Was that supposed to be a joke? Just in case, I laughed. It earned me another look down his nose. I was worm guts again. Then Milo headed down the hall, cradling this dumb bird in his arms.

"Hey! Wait up!" I called, slaloming my way through the crowded corridor. We got to the science lab at the same time.

Instantly, the whole class crowded around Milo, oohing and aahing at the baby chick. Lots of people petted it. It didn't bite any of them.

"He's so cute!" cooed Sheila Martel.

Milo, my soon-to-be best friend, awarded her the worm guts look. "This is a female, of course. A male would occupy an entirely different place in the food chain. You see —"

"What's her name?" interrupted Kelly Marie Ginsberg.

Milo looked mystified. "She doesn't have a name. She's a scientific experiment. You wouldn't name a test tube or a microscope."

"A test tube or a microscope doesn't have a beating heart," Kelly Marie retorted. "Now, what can we call her?"

"Give me a break!" Adam Lurie grumbled.

"How about Chickee?" This from Brendan Walters. He was on the hockey team, too — the goalie — but he wasn't a jerk like Adam and the others. Maybe because he was only in sixth grade.

Kelly Marie's face turned political. "Chickee is sexist."

"Not for a baby chick," I pointed out.

"She won't be a chick forever." Kelly Marie was definitely running the show by this time and, as usual, she had a lot to say. "Can you imagine calling her Chickee when she's a full-grown hen? I know. We'll call her Henrietta!"

"We don't need to call her anything," was Milo's opinion.

But everybody was kitchy-kooing that stupid bird, welcoming "Henrietta" to the lab.

"Hi, Mrs. Baggio," called Kelly Marie. "Meet Henrietta. She's in Milo's project."

"She *is* the project," Milo insisted.

"Look what I've got," the teacher announced grandly. She was holding a milk crate lined with a soft wool blanket. Milo was about to place that lousy bird inside it. But Kelly Marie threw herself in front of him.

"Gently!" she barked, scaring the bird more than Milo. "You're introducing a baby into its new home!"

Milo surrendered the chick and Kelly Marie set it lovingly into the softest folds of the blanket.

"Now, watch." Mrs. Baggio positioned a desk lamp over the box and switched it on.

I couldn't resist. "The chicken is going to do some heavy reading? What? *Egg Digest?*"

I wasn't even surprised when I got the worm guts look from Milo. "It's for the heat, not the light," he explained. "In nature, she would have her mother's body warmth, but we have to improvise. It's kind of like an incubator while the specimen is still a hatchling."

Adam groaned. "We have to buy our own hockey pads, but the school provides an incubator for your chicken if your dad's on TV."

Mrs. Baggio didn't like that. "Adam, that will do. Raising Henrietta will be an excellent learning opportunity for all of us. Milo has generously agreed to let everybody help."

I'd already helped. I gave blood. But for my best friend, bosom buddy, and lifelong chum, Milo — I grabbed the birdseed.

Fade to black . . .

3

RANGERS UPDATE:
CAPTAIN ADAM LURIE REPORTING

That semester I was enrolled in seven classes — math, English, shop, history, gym, French, and chicken. Oh, it still said SCIENCE on the door to the lab, but Mrs. Baggio wasn't teaching anymore. Officially, we were using class time to develop our big projects. In reality, I and twenty-four sixth-grade losers were devoting our lives to a dumb bird named Henrietta.

Can you believe it? Milo put up a job board, and all those numbskulls were breaking their necks to sign up to change the blanket and refill the water dish and feed Henrietta the fine cracked grain she eats.

I don't get it. I mean, even losers have lives, right? I couldn't take a deep breath without thinking about how the Rangers had lost our first three games this season. It was killing me! Yet these little sixth-graders had nothing on their minds beyond performing service to a tweety-bird.

It wasn't exactly fun, either. Chickens don't come toilet trained, so Henrietta went through about five blankets a day. She'd peep and kick and squeak and struggle when someone held her. And nine times out of ten, she got dropped. Before you knew it, she was scrambling across the floor with all twenty-five of us *and* the Bag crawling around on our hands and knees, trying to grab her. Not that we could hold on for very long anyway. I was the only one who could get a real handle on her, because my grip is well trained from taking face-offs in hockey.

"Adam! Not so hard! You'll squash her!" barked Kelly Marie.

"Actually," Milo put in mildly, "according to my research, a hatchling isn't as delicate —"

"How would you like it if a monster fifty times your size squeezed the stuffing out of you?" she stormed.

"That's perfect for my new screenplay!" exclaimed Zachary, rushing off to one of the experiment tables to make notes.

"Look," I told Kelly Marie, "this is Milo's project. If Milo tells me I'm crushing his tweety-bird, I'll stop, but —"

Whack! I can't describe how hard she kicked me —

right across the left shin with her Doc Martens. *And in hockey season!*

I dropped the bird. Kelly Marie made a grab for it but came up empty. Brendan Walters made a flying goalie dive at the fuzzy yellow blur. Nothing.

Peeping like a digital watch, Henrietta hotfooted it across the room at Wayne Gretzky breakaway speed. If anybody had looked in the window at that moment, he'd have thought we were filming a comedy special for the Loser Channel: the whole class throwing themselves at Henrietta, Mrs. Baggio running around with the milk crate, and me, hopping up and down on one foot, yelling about how this injury would slow me down on the ice.

"Keep her away from the window," ordered Milo, still calm. "A draft can be fatal to a hatchling this age."

Well, that was all Kelly Marie had to hear. With a cry of purpose, she hurled herself halfway across the room, landing flat on her stomach between the chick and the window. Henrietta squawked and made a U-turn, scurrying under the table where Zachary still sat making notes. And there was only one thing that could tear Zachary away from his stupid movie — a chance to suck up to Milo Neal.

"Oh, don't worry, Milo. I'll get her." He ducked under the table and reached out an arm. "Come on, Henrietta. Here you go, girl — *OW!!*"

The bird chomped down on his finger. Zachary jumped up like he'd been fired from a rocket launcher.

WHAM! He smashed his head so hard against the underside of the table that everything on top went flying: his movie notes, a couple of pens, and an entire five-pound bag of fine cracked grain.

There was a blizzard of birdseed and half the kids started coughing and sneezing.

"My screenplay!" howled Zachary, hurling himself into the mess after his notes.

At that, he was a good two seconds behind Henrietta. She waded in with both little chicken feet and started chowing. That was when the Bag swooped down and hustled her back into the crate under the warming lightbulb.

"Experiment proceeding on schedule," murmured Milo, updating his project logbook.

Like he didn't notice all the mayhem that was going on around him, courtesy of his chicken.

Picture this five times a day. That was sixth-grade science class.

Our school didn't have a skating rink, so hockey practice was held at the arena in the Community Center.

The guys were a little nervous when I showed up limping, especially since Brendan Walters had an angry red scratch on his face from his big dive at Milo's chick.

"That must be one tough science class," observed

Donald Vincent, who was always called DeeVee for his initials.

"Nah," I grumbled, tying my skates. "I was attacked by an animal rights activist."

Normally, hockey practice was my favorite thing in the world. But working out with this team was getting to be downright painful. We really, truly, honest-to-Pete stank. We were 0 and 3 — and that was only because you can't get negative numbers in hockey. Our last loss was to Hoffman Junior High in Minneapolis, and those slugs are a bunch of country club croquet players who haven't beaten a Ranger team since the seventies. We were hopeless.

Kelly Marie says I'm taking it so hard because I have an obsessed personality. Actually, she doesn't know the half of it! I've been up whole nights sifting through our roster for weak links. At dinner, I can't eat because I'm diagramming our power play in the mashed potatoes. I got to thinking about our problems while I was in the shower last night, and I got so involved that I stood there for forty minutes until the hot water ran out. I can still remember the scream from my dad, who showered after me. That spray must have been ice cold. After all that pondering and wracking my brain and freezing my dad, the question remained: What was wrong with us?

We had talent. Joey Sorrentino and I were the best right wing/center combination in the state. That's when Joey was getting along with his girlfriend, Lynette.

When those two eighth-grade lovebirds were on the rocks, Joey skated on his ankles. Unfortunately for the team, the couple could break up, reunite, and break up again three times a week.

In goal we had Brendan Walters from science class. Normally, I'd hate the idea of a sixth-grader on the team. But Brendan's brother was the Wall, the greatest goalie in Ranger history. Why, last year when the Wall was an eighth-grader, we won the South Minnesota Middle School Championship.

Today, though, Brendan seemed kind of down. "I'd like to quit the team," he confessed. "I let in a lot of soft goals last game. You should look for somebody better."

I couldn't have been more shocked if he'd showed up dressed in a rabbit suit! "But you can't quit! You're the Wall!"

"My brother was the Wall," Brendan insisted. "I'm not my brother."

"But you can be! You *will* be!" I protested. "It's in the genes."

He just sighed and let in another easy shot.

Kapow!

Everybody ducked. Only one thing hit the boards that hard and that was DeeVee's slap shot. It ricocheted three times and still hurt when it hit Coach Crenshaw on the shoulder.

"Vincent, what do you think you're doing?"

DeeVee had a wide, open, slightly stupid face. "Just working on my slap shot, Coach."

"Now tell me something I *don't* know!" snapped the coach. "During passing drill, you were working on your slap shot. Stickhandling is next. What are you going to do? Work on your slap shot?"

DeeVee beamed. "Gee, Coach, could I?"

"No!" bawled Crenshaw.

I should say that the coach was a really nice guy, but he never quite knew what to do with DeeVee. The kid was a talented athlete with tons of potential, but he *would not* practice anything except that slap shot of his. His skating was mediocre, his stickhandling needed work, and the guy didn't have enough patience for checking. All he ever wanted to do was hang around the blue line, waiting to unload that cannon of a slap shot. Which would be fine if it ever went anywhere near the net. But aim wasn't one of DeeVee's strong points, either. He just concentrated on power, and he had plenty of that.

Yet every time DeeVee touched the puck, he was totally positive he was going to score. *And* totally bewildered when he didn't. The rest of us were just happy that he didn't *kill* anybody.

We had rock-solid defensemen — big and tough, even if they did take a few too many penalties. We had real blue-collar wingers who weren't afraid to go into the corners after the puck. We should have been winning.

"It'll come," Coach Crenshaw promised. "Just keep working hard and it'll come."

Yeah, but what year?

Still, we had to put our faith in the coach, and for a very good reason. At the end of the season, the South Minnesota champions always met the best junior high team in Winnipeg, Manitoba, in the biggest game of the year. Well, back in 1959, our Coach Crenshaw was the captain of the Ranger team that beat the Canadians. No one had defeated them before or since. So he knew how to be a winner.

Maybe he could teach it to us.

4

DOWNLOADED FROM THE FILES OF ZACHARY GUSTAFSON

PICNIC OF DEATH

Scene 17

[EXTERIOR SHOT: Pleasant pasture – day]

A troop of GIRL GUIDES with picnic baskets skips gaily across the meadow toward a babbling brook.

GUIDE LEADER

(pointing out birds chirping overhead)

There's a robin redbreast . . .

there's a yellow-bellied sapsucker . . .

LITTLE JUNIE

Oh, look! Butterflies!

LITTLE MAISIE

Look at that tree! What happened to it?

> [POINT-OF-VIEW SHOT: The top of the tree rests on a pile of sawdust around a stump. Something has squeezed the stuffing out of this mighty redwood . . . but what?]

> The field of golden grain begins to undulate.

GUIDE LEADER

It's just the wind, girls . . .

> With a terrible hiss of death, a fifty-foot-long two-headed black-scaled boa constrictor rises out of the wheat field.

> [CLOSE-UP: Spirals whirl within the snake's huge eyes . . . four hypnotizer beams transfix the girls. Two at a time, the twin hideous disgusting heads pick them up and swallow them whole. We see their bodies as lumps traveling all the way down fifty feet of snake.]

I leaned back from my computer, frowning. If there's a problem with my writing style it's that too many of my characters die. That's great for the action but sometimes there's nobody left to be in the rest of the movie. So I deleted the eating part and rewrote:

GUIDE LEADER

Quick, Little Maisie! The flamethrower!

My brow furrowed. There was a believability problem here. Everyone knows a flamethrower won't fit inside even the largest picnic basket. The Hollywood studio executives wouldn't go for it. So:

GUIDE LEADER

Quick, Little Maisie! The grenade!

> LITTLE MAISIE opens her picnic basket, careful not to crease the red-checkered cloth.
>
> [CLOSE-UP: As she opens the Saran Wrap, uncovering the grenade, the lace of her sleeve rides up, revealing her Special Forces tattoo.]

LITTLE MAISIE

(lobbing the grenade into a snake mouth)

Die, reptile scum!

BANG!
It wasn't the sound of the grenade. It was a toy block bouncing off my printer. I wheeled in my swivel chair. My fourteen-month-old baby brother, Dewey, was standing there with his angel face on. Only the halo was missing. Don't believe it. Doomsday Dewey could

hardly walk, and he couldn't talk at all. But he had the destructive power of a kiloton of dynamite.

Still smiling innocently, Doomsday reared back and hurled another block, and this one was headed straight for the computer screen. With speed I didn't know I had, my arm shot out and knocked it down at the last second. Before I could recover, he launched another one. I barely got my foot in the way.

"Cut it out, Dewey —" That's when I saw he was towing his whole bag of blocks. "Mom! *Mom!*"

But it was too late. A barrage of toys was en route to my precious computer. All I could do was dance in front of it, snatching and deflecting, stopping those blocks any way I could, including with my face.

"Zachary, your room is a mess! Why are there blocks all over the floor?"

I pointed an accusing finger at my little brother. "It's Dewey, Mom! He's trying to bust my computer!"

She picked up Doomsday and scowled at me. "Do you honestly expect me to believe that this little baby attacked you and your computer with blocks?" The kid's arms hung limply at his sides. He looked like he couldn't *lift* a block, let alone throw like Greg Maddux.

"He's not a baby," I muttered. "He's a very short terrorist."

"You have an attitude problem," my mother accused. "Fighting with your brother, fighting at school —"

Huh? "I haven't been fighting at school!"

Her eyes narrowed. "Then how do you explain that bump on your head?"

"I was under the table, trying to catch a runaway chicken —"

She cut me off. "Now, *really,* Zachary. I know your imagination is important to your writing, but please don't use it on me."

She stormed out, with Doomsday smiling at me over her shoulder.

"And clean up those blocks!" That part came from halfway down the stairs.

I checked over my computer. There was a little scratch where the block hit the printer but everything else was okay. Still, it was pretty upsetting to think that my writing career almost got smashed. I mean, how could I sit down and describe a fifty-foot-long boa constrictor blowing to pieces, with charred intestines and hunks of snake flesh flying all over the Girl Guides, when I was in a bad mood?

Great. Four o'clock on a Friday afternoon and already my weekend was shot.

Then it came to me like a bolt out of the blue. How do you lift yourself up when your spirits are down? You hang out with friends! And who was a better friend of mine than my good buddy, Milo Neal?

To be honest, we weren't yet quite as close as I'd hoped we'd be. That's probably because Milo was so busy with The Chicken from the Black Lagoon. Actually, he didn't really know who I was, which presented a problem: How could he introduce me to his famous L.A.-connected father if he didn't remember my name?

That was all the more reason Milo and I needed some quality time together. I was knocking on his door in three minutes flat.

I recognized Mrs. Neal from her pictures in the paper when she moved back to town after the divorce.

"Hi," I greeted her. "I'm here to see Milo."

"Oh, Milo's still at school," she told me. "He's working late on his science project."

Even now that stupid chicken was messing me up.

Then she pitched me a fat one. "Are you a friend of Milo's?"

I gave it a home-run swing. "Oh, yeah!" I said quickly, "I'm Zachary, probably his best friend in the whole school." That might not have even been a lie. "We had plans to get together today, but I guess he got wrapped up in our project." Okay, that *was* a lie, but thanks to Mrs. Baggio, everybody in the class was sort of Milo's partner.

She looked worried. "Oh, dear. Maybe I should call the school."

"Oh, that's okay, Mrs. Neal. I'll just walk along and see if I can catch him on the way home."

I spotted Milo a couple of blocks from the school. He was stooped over to adjust the blanket in Henrietta's milk crate. I came up behind and awarded him a best-friend slap on the back.

"Whoa!!" Shocked, he snapped back up like an elastic and glared at me through Bertrand St. Rene glasses that were slightly askew. It was worm guts time again.

"I watched your dad's show last night," I babbled, trying to smooth things over. "Well, not exactly, because my family's too cheap to spring for the Science Channel, so it was scrambled. But I heard most of it and it sounded great."

Milo picked up Henrietta's milk crate and started walking toward his house. I trotted along beside him. "How come you're taking the chicken home?" I asked.

"A whole weekend is too long to leave the specimen on her own," he explained. "She needs fresh food and water at least twice a day."

I peeked under the blanket. A baleful eye and a loud squawk warned me away. "Very cute," I totally lied.

"A chicken is not cute," Milo explained patiently. "A chicken is a chicken. It is not a pet. It exists purely to occupy a space in the food chain."

I looked at my hands, which were dotted with peck marks from guess who. "I think my fingers must occupy the space directly below that."

Milo nodded grudgingly. "I know it looks like the specimen hates you, but she doesn't possess the brain-power to single you out."

We were at the Neals' front walk. Milo seemed pretty weirded out by the fact that I followed him onto the porch instead of leaving.

"Well, good-bye," he said hopefully.

Suddenly, the door was flung open and Milo's mother was beaming at us. "Zachary! I see you found him. Milo, why didn't you tell me your friend would be stopping by?" She was so psyched about me that it seemed pretty plain she'd been worrying about her son being lonely in his new town. You wouldn't believe the look on Milo's face when she hauled the two of us inside for these great chili nachos she'd whipped up.

I was thinking, I'm in! I mean, surely it was just a short step from nachos with Milo to Victor Neal setting up a meeting between me and the president of Universal Studios. I could almost see their special-effects department building my fifty-foot-long boa constrictor.

Then the doorbell rang, and in a few seconds Mrs. Neal was calling, "Milo, it's another one of your friends."

I glared at him accusingly. But poor Milo looked so dumbfounded that I instantly forgave him for betraying our friendship.

Into the kitchen burst none other than Kelly Marie. She breezed past us and knelt over the milk crate.

"There's my little Henrietta! Hello, sweetie!" She looked daggers at Milo. "What's the big idea of taking her out of the classroom without ever thinking that the people who love her might be worried?"

Milo spread his arms wide. "The specimen couldn't be left at school all weekend."

"That's it!" Kelly Marie snatched up the milk carton. "She's coming with me!"

Milo was completely mystified. "Why?"

"Because at your house she's nothing more than a specimen, but at my house she's a guest!"

I picked up Milo's line. "A chicken is not a guest. A chicken is a chicken."

She was ready for me. "Shut up, Zachary."

Milo looked worried. "Hmmm."

I frowned. That was the best Victor Neal's son could do? Hmmm? What about, "Get out of here, you big-mouthed pain in the butt, and get your own chicken, and don't come back until *your* dad stars in *his* own TV show!" Instead, he said, "I have to maintain constant contact with my experiment."

"Fine," agreed Kelly Marie. She grabbed the notepad on the kitchen counter and scribbled her name and phone number. "Call me anytime," she added, slapping the paper in front of Milo. And out she went, carrying the milk crate with her.

That really burned me up. Here I was, Milo's best friend. But all Kelly Marie had to do was waltz in here, crab around for three minutes, and presto, he had her phone number. Quickly, I tore off another sheet and wrote down my number.

Milo was giving me the worm guts treatment. He was going to throw it out. I knew it.

If he wasn't my best friend, I'd really hate that guy.

Fade to black . . .

5 🐔

EXPERIMENT NOTES: MILO NEAL
10/28

> Did you ever get the feeling that there's something going on and everybody knows about it except you? And that something, if you could just find out what it was, would unlock so many mysteries?

> Like why Mrs. Baggio has dropped everything so the whole class can participate in my simple science experiment. Everyone else is doing a proj. What's so special about a chicken?

> Or why that girl Kelly Marie bulldozed her way into my house and walked off with my subject. {It's hard to believe these Minnesotans can't seem to accept that this is a specimen, not their darling Henrietta. They wouldn't adopt a lab rat as a pet?!}

> And Zachary Gustafson. I can't guess what's driving him, but I know *he's* driving me crazy. My father has an expression: "He sticks to you like ugly on an ape." ZG = a human boomerang; no matter how many times you throw him away, he always comes back. Now my mother thinks he and I = best friends.

> Things were a lot simpler in California. {I miss my dad. But I know if I lived with him in Los Angeles, I'd miss my mom just as much. Of course, the weather would be better. This town = deep freeze.}

> I had misgivings about releasing my experiment to KMG. Sure enough, on Monday, subj. had undergone a 6% increase in body mass.

Even an idiot could spot the size difference. And one did.

"No way that's Henrietta!" ZG accused. "I'll bet she croaked on you and you're trying to cover it up by buying a new chicken!"

> But then subj. pecked his hand so hard it bled, which was better I.D. than a social security card. It was still her, all right. {How could a chicken know to hate one person and not another?/further study req'd. Although sometimes I think chomping a hunk out of ZG's hand would make me feel better, too.}

"You overfed her," I accused KMG. "She's fat."

> KMG responds to an undeniable truth by going on the offensive.

"My mom was late for her PTO meeting so she could

drive me to the Farmers' Union to buy birdseed infant starter mash. I fed her *what* you said. I fed her *when* you said."

"But not *how much* I said," I retorted.

"She ate it, didn't she?" snapped KMG, eyes shooting sparks. "If Henrietta's growing, it's because she's thriving on love, which is more than she could do at your house. You don't even like her!"

I responded, for at least the tenth time, "There's nothing to like or dislike. This is a science project. Yours is on recycling. Do you 'like' old newspapers?"

KMG leaned into my face like a Marine drill sergeant. "Recycling old newspapers cleans up the environment, which makes the ecosystem a better place for living creatures like Henrietta! So yes, I *love* old newspapers!"

> Arguing with KMG = banging your head against the wall. It's noisy, painful, and pointless.

"You know what your problem is, Milo Neal?" she went on. "Too much brain and not enough heart. It may be good science but it's definitely not living."

"However the size increase happened," I sighed, "I think it's just about time to stop treating her like a hatchling."

"What are we supposed to treat her like?" growled Adam L. "The Homecoming Queen?"

"A pullet," I replied. "That's the next stage in the life cycle. She remains a pullet until she becomes a full-fledged hen."

"What's so different about being a pullet?" asked Brendan Walters.

"Well, for starters," I replied, "she can't live in that old crate anymore. She needs space to move around."

I had noticed Mrs. Baggio quivering with excitement throughout all of this. Finally, her enthusiasm bubbled over the surface.

"I have such a wonderful surprise for everyone!" She threw open an equipment closet and there stood a bale of chicken wire and two bags of sawdust. "We're going to build a chicken coop!"

"Mrs. Baggio!" I said, shocked. "The specimen couldn't possibly survive the harsh winter outside!"

"Oh, not outside," Mrs. B assured me. "Right here in the lab. There's plenty of room. We'll just move these tables, stack those chairs in the corner — come on, people. Let's all get to work."

> I wonder if all new students get this kind of special treatment. Here I was, worrying about finding a bigger box, and the whole class, including the teacher, was building luxury accommodations for my experiment. {This definitely wouldn't happen in California. Maybe it = small-town hospitality/further study req'd.}

The coop took up the entire southeast corner of the room. Mrs. B stapled four-foot-high chicken fencing to the south wall and strung it across to the east wall. That made a triangular enclosure, which we filled with sawdust. Yes, I helped. Nobody asked me to, but I felt it was only fair that I pitch in with my own science proj.

When I leaned over to fix some tangled wire, I distinctly heard AL mutter, "I got a week of detention for a gum wrapper on the art room floor. But forty pounds of sawdust is no problem if it's for Milo's chicken!"

> Can't he see it's not my fault? It's Mrs. B!

"Don't listen to him, Milo, pal," whispered ZG. "He's just bummed because his hockey team stinks. By the way, I forgot to thank you for having me over on Friday. What a great time that was! A real party!"

> A party? Sitting in the kitchen eating my mother's nachos?

"Look, Henrietta," warbled KMG. "Look at your lovely new home!" She lifted the specimen out of the milk crate and placed her inside the pen. The pullet darted around, exploring her new territory.

The whole class broke into applause.

"Take a bow, Milo!" crowed Mrs. B.

> I must have been bright red.

Somebody, probably AL, muttered the word, "conceited."

> People always say Californians are strange. They've obviously never been to St. Martin, Minnesota.

6

RANGERS UPDATE:
CAPTAIN ADAM LURIE REPORTING

I never planned to get stuck with the chicken. It was partially my own fault — kind of like my punishment for fraternizing with a loser. Not just any loser, but the Grand Master High Exalted Lord of the Losers, screenwriting's answer to toe jam, Zachary Gustafson.

Okay, I was cracking on the guy. Who could resist? I was hanging out with Barbara Falconi after school on Friday, killing time before the Rangers game, when Zachary came along. To my amazement, he was lugging Henrietta in a Macy's bag with airholes.

So I yelled, "Run for your life, Henrietta! He's taking you to the river!"

"I am not!" The dweeb was really insulted. "For your information, my good friend Milo has entrusted me with his specimen."

I was bug-eyed. "All weekend?" I couldn't imagine the amount of nagging it must have taken to swing that one.

"Well, just for tonight," Zachary admitted. "But when Milo comes over and sees how happy she is, he'll let me keep her until Monday morning. I've got an old rabbit pen that's perfect for a chicken."

"Why can't Milo the Great look after his own tweety-bird?" I asked.

"He can," Superloser replied. "But half the class volunteered. Milo picked me because he and I are such good friends."

I was genuinely curious. "Why are you doing this? Everybody knows you hate that chicken, and it's pretty obvious the chicken hates you."

"That's all in the past," Zachary explained. "Henrietta and I are getting along just fine now. See?" The dweeb opened up the sack to show us how he was stroking Henrietta's feathers. With a squawk of outrage, the bird rose out of the bag and went for Zachary with a vengeance, claws slashing at his face. He jumped so fast that he let go of the handle. And Henrietta was on the loose, hop-scrambling along the faded terrazzo floor.

"Oh, no! *Oh, no!*" howled Zachary. He took off like Wile E. Coyote after the Road Runner. Barbara and I were hot on his heels.

"Look out!" cried Barbara. She could see what I saw — the custodian's rolling mop pail directly in

Superloser's path. All Zachary could see was Milo's chicken, his big chance to suck up, getting away.

He galloped down the hall, wailing like a banshee. His high-stepping foot came down with a splash right in the bucket. But amazingly, Zachary didn't fall. Instead, his momentum started the wheeled bucket rolling. He stood there, poised like a figure skater, his free leg held high, while the mop caddy picked up speed. He zoomed past the art room, past the drinking fountain, and past Henrietta.

CRASH!

Do I need to spell it out? No hallway goes on forever. I grabbed Henrietta, and Barbara ran over to Zachary, who was lying in a pool of dirty suds by the wall he'd just smashed into.

Eyes tightly shut, he felt around the wetness and whispered, "Is it blood?" Then, a little louder, "And more important — is it *chicken* blood?"

I had to laugh. "The chicken's alive and so are you." I reached out my free hand and hauled him to his feet. He looked a little unsteady.

"I think we should take him to the nurse's office," Barbara decided.

"Aw, he's okay." I turned to the victim. "Aren't you, Zack?"

Zachary replied, and I quote, " 'Doomsday, stay away from my computer.' "

"Well, I'm taking him!" said Barbara firmly. And she started off toward the stairwell, leading the dazed Zachary.

I held up Henrietta, who was trying to wriggle her way out of my grasp. "But what am I supposed to do with the bird?"

She shrugged. "Find Milo and give her back."

"But I've got a *game* to get to! Coach wants us in the locker room in twenty minutes!"

She scowled at me. "Don't be so selfish. Who cares about hockey when somebody could be really hurt?"

I do! But the heavy doors thumped shut and I was alone in the hallway.

"Way to go, bird," I growled at Henrietta. "Thanks a lot."

It took forever to wrestle her back into the bag. Then I started running all over the school, looking for the great Milo. No Milo. No *anybody*. Most of the kids were probably over at the Community Center to get good seats for the game. It would be crowded, since our opponents were our crosstown rivals from North Middle School, the Kings. So this was kind of a home game for both teams.

The lab was my last resort. Maybe I could dump Henrietta in her coop and track down California Boy later. But the door was locked. Even the Bag had left for the day! If I got benched for being late, I was going to hit Milo Neal so hard that he would land back in Beverly Hills, or Bel Air, or wherever those famous California-types lived. If he was such a big shot, why couldn't he hire a butler to look after his chicken?

The hall clock clicked as loud as a pistol shot. It was 3:58 and I was supposed to be in the dressing room in *two minutes!*

I sprinted to the nurse's office. It was deserted.

What kind of a crummy rip-off school *was* this? What if I had elephantiasis and needed medical attention?

I looked up. It was four o'clock. I was officially late. I made the only decision I could make under the circumstances: Henrietta was going to a hockey game.

If there's a world record for a half-mile race carrying twenty pounds of hockey equipment and a chicken, I shattered it.

Coach Crenshaw was really mad. "I guess the captain of a last-place team can just toddle in whenever he feels like it! What's the big idea, Lurie?"

Blue-faced and gasping, I could only point to the shopping bag.

"That's no excuse!" roared the coach. "I don't care what's in that —"

And then the pullet's head poked out of one of the airholes.

"Henrietta!" exclaimed Brendan.

"A chicken?!" cried Coach Crenshaw in disbelief.

"It's Milo Neal's science project!" I wheezed, throwing on my equipment.

"Yeah, but why did you bring it *here?*"

"It's a long story," I managed, lacing my skates at the speed of light. "There was no one else around. Maybe you can find someone else to take her."

"I'm the coach, not the chicken-sitter. Besides, it's time for our warmup." He clapped for attention. "Everybody on the ice."

The guys stood up on their skates and clattered out of the dressing room. I picked up the bag and got in line.

Coach Crenshaw goggled. "Where do you think you're going with that?"

"I'll leave her on the bench during the game!" I promised.

"Forget it, Lurie!" he said stoutly. "I trust you enough to accept your word that the animal has to be here. But no way is it going to be our trainer! The chicken stays in the dressing room!"

I admit it; I went to pieces. "Oh, please, Coach! If somebody opens the door and this stupid bird gets loose, we'll never see it again. It'll get lost — or trampled — or run over by the Zamboni. And Mrs. Baggio *loves* this chicken! I mean, Milo and the chicken are her whole life! If I lose it, I'll flunk sixth-grade science *again!* And then I'm off the team for sure!"

Good old Coach Crenshaw. He took pity on me. "Okay, but no feathers in the Gatorade."

"Thanks, Coach! You're the greatest!"

The crowd turned out to be mostly Kings fans — probably because they were having a great year, and we were 0 and 5. The South kids who did show up had a good laugh at the sight of me skating the warmup with a Macy's bag. The other team stared at me like I was nuts.

"Doing your Christmas shopping early?" the Kings' captain sneered at me as we passed near center ice.

A tiny chicken leg reached out of the bag and took a swipe at the guy's shin pads.

The big baby started hollering for the ref. "Hey, he slashed me!"

"I did not!"

"Did so!"

We *did-not-did-so*'ed at each other for a while, until finally the referee said, "Let's see what's in the bag."

"It's . . . extra pucks."

"Then you won't mind me checking them out," said the man.

In resignation, I opened the bag wide.

"A chicken?!" cried the Kings' captain in disbelief.

"Is it rubber?" demanded the referee suspiciously. Throwing rubber chickens on the ice was an old-time hockey gag — one that was banned in middle-school play.

"No, it's real," I admitted.

The referee considered this. "Is it your mascot?"

Sue me — I said yes. It was easier than trying to explain.

I wedged the Macy's bag between Steve Tenorio and Lafayette Hughes and went to take the opening face-off.

The Rangers usually had no trouble beating North Middle School. But we were so lousy and this was the best Kings team in years, so we were considered the underdogs.

I won the face-off and got the puck to Joey, who found a streaking DeeVee with a beautiful pass. It should have been a cinch; he had a wide-open path to the net. But instead, DeeVee decided it was time for his patented slap shot. He put on the brakes in a shower of snow and raised his stick so high that he nearly overbalanced and almost fell flat on his back.

I heard Coach Crenshaw scream, "Vincent, don't you dare!"

But it was already too late.

POW!

The shot was as hard as a bullet — and twenty feet above the net. It bounced off the balcony and busted a light on the scoreboard in a shower of sparks. It came back down to the ice just past center, where it started a three-man breakaway for the Kings. Poor Brendan didn't have a prayer. 1–0, North Middle School. Exactly eighteen seconds had ticked off the clock.

"Vincent — you're *benched!*" howled Coach Crenshaw.

"I had to take it, Coach!" DeeVee pleaded. "It was a sure goal!"

The coach waved wildly at the scoreboard. "Is that a one on *our* side? No! It's a one on *their* side!"

"I'll get it next time, Coach! I promise!"

"There isn't going to be a next time, because you'll be *riding the pine!*"

A disconsolate DeeVee sat down to flank Henrietta, and Laffy Hughes came on to join our line.

It was a tough game. The Kings led 2–zip at the end of the first period, and 4–1 by the second intermission. I have to say that two of those goals were pretty soft. The Wall was having another shaky outing in net, and we were heading for 0 and 6 in a hurry.

Coach Crenshaw tried to get us revved up in the locker room, but Henrietta kept squawking and rustling the bag, so he couldn't get everybody's attention.

"If they beat you, they beat you!" roared the coach. "But don't beat yourselves!"

"Maybe she needs more airholes," suggested Brendan.

"Maybe she's hungry," put in Joey.

"Maybe your coach is talking to you!" howled Crenshaw.

At that moment, the buzzer sounded, calling us back to the ice.

Our fans — those who hadn't left yet — were silent. All the noise in the arena was being made by the North Middle School supporters — cheers, applause, chants —

and what was that other sound? I looked around in confusion. It was coming from the Kings' bench — a high-pitched warbling chatter.

It hit me in a moment of exquisite humiliation. "They're making chicken noises!" I howled in outrage. "They're clucking at us!"

Joey leaned over the boards. *"Shut up!"* he bellowed, which only made the Kings warble louder. Now the noise was mixed with raucous laughter. Worse, they began flapping their arms. That was when Henrietta wiggled halfway out of the bag, probably to check out the clucking.

It put the Kings over the top. They were practically berserk with laughter.

"The Chicken Rangers!"

"Drumsticks on ice!"

"Ranger Fricasee!"

"Why did the Rangers cross the road?"

I have to say the chicken took it better than we did. I was in a blind rage, and the third period hadn't even started yet.

The Kings' captain was still laughing as he skated up to take the face-off. "Cock-a-doodle-do!"

"That's a rooster, you moron!" I exploded. "Ours is a baby hen! A girl!" I was so infuriated that I forgot to take a swipe at the face-off. He took the puck and I lowered my shoulder and let him have it — a beautiful check, all nice and legal. He went straight up and took a swan dive over my shoulder. But I wasn't there to see him come down. I grabbed the puck and charged down the ice. Just past the blue line I hit Lafayette with a perfect drop pass. Then I swooped in and screened the goalie, and Laffy found the corner of the net with a hard shot along the ice. 4–2, Kings.

From then on, it turned into a grudge match. They threw everything they had at us, and believe it or not, we threw it right back in their faces! Steve had just scored to pull us within one, when Lynette Martinez showed up at our bench.

"Where's Joey? I have to talk to Joey!"

Coach Crenshaw stared at her. *"Now?!"*

I pointed to the ice. "He's double-shifting."

As if on cue, a large Kings defenseman smashed Joey up against the boards with a savage body check.

Lynette rushed over. "Joey! *Joey!"*

Joey's helmet was pressed against the glass. He mouthed the word, "What?"

"Joey, I was wrong!" Lynette said emotionally. "I was wrong and you were right!"

"No, *I* was wrong!" Joey shouted into the dirty fiberglass.

"I was the one who was wrong!" shrieked Lynette, and for a moment, I thought they were going to start fighting about it. "I'm awful," she went on. "I'm the worst girlfriend in the world."

"You're the *best!"* Joey cried.

"The *worst!* The *worst!*" Remember, soap opera fans, all this was happening in the middle of the play! "I'm so, *so* sorry, and I want to get back together again!"

"*Yeah?!*" Joey's face beamed like a Christmas tree the first time the lights are turned on. He shook off his checker, kicked the puck free, and galloped down the ice with it, throwing off Kings with a stiff arm.

"Go, man!" I screamed, but Joey didn't need any help from me. He charged the net like a rhino. The goalie went down, smothering the puck under a pad. But Joey kept on digging with his stick. With a cry of pure determination, he muscled the puck loose and fired it into the net. Tie game.

You could almost feel the earth move as we all leaped up to cheer, coming down on our skates at the same moment. Lynette climbed over the boards and made a joyful run at Joey. She had to be restrained by the referee.

"But that's my *boyfriend* who scored that goal!" she wailed.

"Later!" The man escorted her off the ice. "There's still two minutes to play!"

They must have been the longest two minutes in history. Both teams fought exhaustion to break the deadlock. Even DeeVee got another chance to play, as the coaches searched their lineups for fresh legs. With thirty-one seconds remaining, the score was still 4–4. My whole body felt numb, but I was exhilarated. After five terrible losses, it looked like the Rangers were going to come out with a tie against a tough opponent.

Then things started to go horribly wrong. Joey forgot to drop back to cover for a pinching defenseman. DeeVee missed a pass, and the Kings got the puck. I made a U-turn to help out on defense — and that was when I caught sight of our bench.

In all the excitement over the final seconds, my teammates were on their feet, following the action. No one was watching the Macy's bag, and Henrietta must have crawled loose and climbed up onto the boards. There she sat like a hood ornament, spectating along with everybody else.

The dilemma almost tore me in two. Did I try to prevent the Kings from scoring the winning goal or make sure that Henrietta didn't get away? It should have been no contest, right? Hockey versus a stupid chicken belonging to the town snob in my least favorite class. But it must have been temporary insanity — I zoomed toward the bench.

I thought the coach's eyes were going to pop out of his head. "Are you *crazy,* Lurie?! Get back in the play!"

"The bird!" I shouted. "Somebody grab the bird!"

Laffy got his arms around Henrietta just as the Kings' captain unleashed a blistering shot from point-blank range.

"I can't look!" bawled Coach Crenshaw.

CLANG! The drive hit the goalpost and ricocheted into the corner. There was a mad scramble for the puck. DeeVee got there first and golfed it out past our blue line.

At first, I couldn't understand why the whole team was screaming in my face. Then reality sunk in: The puck was bouncing toward me — *and I was all alone behind the play!*

I snatched the puck just before center ice and took off. It was every hockey player's dream — a clean breakaway with ten seconds to play in a tie game. By the time I crossed the blue line I was flying, the roar of the crowd powering me like rocket fuel. I sizzled in on net, raising my stick for a slap shot. Then, at the last second, I pulled the puck to my backhand and flipped it past the goalie's blocker into the net. Final score 5–4, Rangers.

It was a miracle Henrietta didn't get crushed during the celebration. I sure did when my teammates cleared the bench and mobbed me. They lifted me up onto their shoulders and carried me into the dressing room. It was a good thing I was wearing a helmet because my head smacked into that door frame pretty hard. It was a great moment.

Coach Crenshaw seemed just as excited as we were. He was pounding guys on the back, shouting, "See what you can do when you put your minds to it?"

I sat down and slumped against the wall, savoring the thrill. "You're so right, Coach. It's hard to believe we were the same Rangers who lost five in a row."

The mood turned serious as we all thought about our season.

Joey spoke up. "Well, what was different about this game over all the others?"

I looked around. As I scrutinized my teammates' faces, I realized that all eyes had come to rest on the Macy's bag.

"Now, wait a minute!" the coach pulled up short. "Surely you don't think —" He stared at us in disbelief. "The chicken doesn't skate! Right? You won that game! *You!*"

But he had lost his audience. The South Middle School Rangers were focused on the shopping bag and, peering out through a rip, Henrietta.

7

"PSYCHOLOGY TALK"
BY KELLY MARIE GINSBERG

I think I have a pretty good understanding of psychology. I mean, when Karen Van Dusen had her accident-prone day — ran into the soccer goalpost, set fire to the science lab, and pushed an entire shopping cart of filmstrips and herself down the back stairs — I wasn't fooled. It was an attention-getting device because her older sister had just become a model, and Karen has a face like a Rottweiler. I read people.

It's just like when Joey Sorrentino and Lynette Martinez started trading insults and fighting. Everybody else said, "Separate these two before they kill each other." But I knew that deep down there was a real attraction. And when Joey flushed Lynette's best barrette down the toilet, and she responded by pushing him through the plate-glass window of the art room, I knew it was true love. Psychology.

I cured Sophie Tisdale's fear of lipstick, predicted the end of Adam Lurie's scoring slump, and even helped Horace Maminsky get over his strange obsession with peanut butter.

So why couldn't I figure out Milo Neal?

I didn't know whether to kiss him or strangle him. Seriously! He was the one who brought us Henrietta. Yet he insisted on treating her like an animal!

And for a guy who was supposed to be a genius, how could he be stupid enough to entrust Henrietta to Zachary for the weekend?

"Are you crazy?" I bellowed on Monday morning when I found out. "She *hates* Zachary!"

He rolled his eyes at me. "A chicken doesn't have the intelligence —"

"Henrietta is *not* stupid!" I cut him off. "She's a perceptive, sensitive creature, and if she hates Zachary Gustafson, then it must be for a good reason. Maybe chickens have a special radar that can detect a maniac. Have you ever read those sick screenplays of his? Why couldn't you give her to *me?*"

"She went with you last weekend," he offered lamely.

I made a face. "Oh, I get it. She doesn't have the brains to hate somebody, but she finds it unacceptable to receive the same hospitality two weekends in a row. Half the class wanted Henrietta. Why *him?*"

Milo gave me a sheepish look. "I thought maybe if I gave him a little responsibility, he might stop calling me and coming over to my house."

Pretty good psychology, if I say so myself. You break down a patient's defenses and he tells you what he's *really* thinking. I was about to congratulate Milo on this breakthrough when I caught sight of Zachary at the far end of the hall.

"Follow me!" I tossed over my shoulder as I sprinted over to Zachary. Henrietta *wasn't* with him.

"Oh, hi," he greeted. "What's up?"

"All right," I confronted him. "Where is she?"

He looked blank. "Where is who?"

"Who?" I struggled for control. "Abraham Lincoln. Sonic the Hedgehog. *Henrietta,* you dolt! You were in charge of her this weekend!"

"Oh," he said with a nervous laugh, "that all got canceled. I had a little accident, so I couldn't do it." He showed me the remnants of a small bruise on his cheek.

"Well, who's got her now?" I persisted.

"How should I know?"

I stared in horror. "Who took Henrietta when you got hurt?"

He shrugged. "Nurse Jansen brought me over to Emergency and then my parents drove me straight home after that."

I don't know why I kicked him so hard. I made a

mental note to analyze my dreams that night to figure it out.

Milo finally made it to the scene. I turned on him. "I told you it was nuts to entrust Henrietta to this flake! He *lost* her!"

Instantly, Milo looked to Zachary, who nodded, studying his sneakers.

Milo was appalled. "When I phoned on Saturday night, you told me the specimen was one hundred percent."

Zachary struggled to save himself. "Well, she might have been. You know, wherever she was." He hung his head in shame. "I'm sorry, Milo."

Milo was visibly upset. I have to admit I felt some satisfaction seeing Milo the Unflappable show some feeling.

"This is terrible!" he exclaimed. "My experiment is in danger of being compromised!"

"I'll compromise your face if anything happens to Henrietta!" I promised darkly.

"Maybe . . ." I began. That's when I heard the cheering. It seemed to be coming from the cafeteria.

"*Give me a T —*" hollered somebody.

"*T!!*" came a chorus of voices.

"*Give me an A —*"

"*A!!*"

"*What does it spell?*"

"*Henrietta!!*" chanted the group.

We raced past the breakfast line and stopped dead.

Atop a cafeteria table perched none other than Adam Lurie, holding the shopping bag aloft. I couldn't see Henrietta, but I could make out the impression of her sweet little beak pressed against the Macy's logo. Adam's hockey buddies and a handful of others made up the crowd.

I looked daggers up at Adam. "You had her all along?"

He shrugged down at us. "Zack was hurt; someone had to take Henrietta. My mom and I made a coop out of a couple of old hockey nets in the garage." He added, "Okay, Milo?"

"Acceptable —" Milo began.

"You should have *called* me!" I cut him off. "Henrietta hardly knows you! She must have been terrified — in your dark, dingy garage, surrounded by total strangers all weekend! You had no right to do it!"

"Hey," said Joey, "she's *our* mascot."

"Mascot?!" It came from me, Milo, and Zachary.

"We finally won last Friday, and Henrietta was on the bench with us. So —" the way Adam said it, you'd think it was the most normal, sensible thing in the world "— she has to be there for the rest of the season." The other Rangers nodded in agreement.

"Adam," said Milo seriously, "as an athlete, you must know that makes absolutely no scientific sense."

"Hey, man," said Steve sharply, "you don't mess with a winning streak."

"What winning streak?" I exploded. "It was only one game!"

"It doesn't matter!" Adam insisted. "If you lace your skates wrong before a big win, you do it that way forever! If your mom wears polka dots in the bleachers, it's law! If you step into your jockstrap left-leg-first, that becomes the next amendment to the Constitution! And that includes keeping a tweety-bird on the bench!"

Have I mentioned my theory about how hockey players are like cave dwellers crawling through the mud pit of a thousand monster-truck rallies? What — I mean, *what* could you say to a speech like that?

8 🐔

DOWNLOADED FROM THE FILES
OF ZACHARY GUSTAFSON

THE BRAIN EATERS

Scene 11

[INTERIOR: Burning building – night]

FIREFIGHTERS hack down the flaming door and DE-TECTIVE JEFFERS leaps heroically through the fire to where STEVE lies dying of 34 broken bones, internal bleeding, head wounds, and tonsilitis.

JEFFERS

Are you all right?

STEVE

(gasping for breath)

Forget about me! I'm a goner! You have to stop . . .
him . . .

JEFFERS

You mean . . . the brain-eating psycho-monster?

STEVE

I know his secret identity.

JEFFERS

What is it?

STEVE

(beckoning him closer)

To catch the brain-eating psycho-monster, just look for a
big . . . a big . . .

JEFFERS

A big what?

But it's too late. STEVE's eyes roll back in his head and
he dies.

CUT TO:

The BRAIN-EATING PSYCHO-MONSTER, fleeing
through the streets, his six insect legs showing under
his trench coat. He spreads terror to all who see his repulsive pustule-covered praying mantis head.

He approaches the university science lab, home of

some of the biggest and most delicious brains in the
city.

Hungrily, the MONSTER licks his green lips with a
tongue coated with glowing acid. Then, before our
eyes, he mutates into his secret identity —

Which was . . .

What?

I stared at my computer screen in total despair. Right
in the middle of the most exciting, pivotal scene in my
screenplay, I had writer's block. I didn't have the slightest idea what the brain-eating psycho-monster's secret
identity should be.

This was terrible! I'd never had writer's block in my
whole life. And just when Milo and I were starting to hit
it off, too. Oh, sure, he was still pretty steamed about last
weekend. I think his exact words were, "Go away. I
never want to see you again for the rest of my life."
Actually, I was pretty impressed I managed to get such an
emotional reaction from a quiet guy like Milo. That was
one of the reasons I knew we were going to be so close.

I chewed on my pen. I opened and closed every single drawer in my desk. I chewed on my pen again. This
time the cap broke and I got ink in my mouth. Several
minutes of hacking and spitting later, I was no closer to
the solution to my problem.

I was checking myself for permanent blueness when
I caught a glimpse of a darting shape in the bathroom

mirror. My throat seized. It was Doomsday — *headed straight for my room!*

"Dew – ey!!!" I made a desperate sprint across the hall and burst into my doorway. Doomsday already had his tiny baby hand cocked back, ready to throw a size-D battery at my computer.

I left my feet just as he launched the battery. With a flailing hand I slapped it away, at the same time leaping over my little brother and interposing myself between him and the desk.

But Doomsday still had plenty of ammo. He must have raided the junk drawer of my dad's desk. I blocked the fountain pen with my left hand and deflected the letter opener with my right. The chess queen made a nasty bump on my knee. The magnet and the pencil sharpener were a painful one-two punch as I stopped them with my chest. I won't even mention where the paperweight got me.

I had no choice but to wait until Doomsday ran out of projectiles, since I didn't dare yell for my mother. She'd blame this all on me, just like last Friday. I mean, *everybody* steps on a mop caddy and rolls into a wall. It happens to millions of people. But Mom — my own flesh and blood! — accused me of fighting and banned me from my computer for three days. It totally threw my screenplay off schedule and probably contributed to my writer's block. I couldn't risk it again.

So I took the heat. *And* the pain. *And* the white-out

bottle in the face. Finally, the last protractor ricocheted off my solar plexus.

"Ha!" I snorted. "What are you going to do now?"

Doomsday scrunched up his baby face and started to howl.

Mom was on the scene in a nanosecond. "Zachary Gustafson, how *dare* you pick on your little brother! And what happened to your room? It's a pigsty!"

"It's a battlefield!"

"It's a disgrace!"

She folded her arms. I knew I was toast. I made a feeble last-ditch effort. "It was Dewey, Mom! Honest!"

But even as I tried to defend myself, Mom strode purposefully over to my PC and pulled the plug. "This will cost you a week away from your computer, young man."

"A whole week? That's too long! It's not fair! You're messing with my creativity!" But at least I had my deadline, just like the big-time screenwriters. Seven days to figure out the secret identity of the brain-eating psychomonster.

". . . and finally, in hockey action on Saturday," came Mr. Delong's voice over the PA system Monday morning, "the Rangers defeated St. Cloud by a score of eight to five. That's four in a row for our Rangers. Don't forget to come to the pep rally after school today. The team will be there — *and* Henrietta."

All through the halls of the school I could hear the

cheering. Didn't it figure? My two least favorite things — the hockey team and Milo's stupid chicken — were turning into the heroes of the year. Coupled with my writer's block, it was pretty depressing.

I just so happened to run into Milo by standing in front of his locker for twenty minutes. He tried to walk away but, like any good friend, I stayed loyal. I followed him all the way to the science room.

"I had a nice conversation with your mom on Saturday." Actually, while I'd talked on the phone to Mrs. Neal, in the background I could hear my dearest friend hissing, "Tell him I'm not here! Tell him I've gone out! Tell him I moved to Europe!"

He blushed. "I was kind of busy," he mumbled, throwing open the lab door. He probably wanted to slam it in my face, but that was impossible. The lab was jam-packed with people. Milo crammed himself in behind a tall eighth-grader.

Lafayette Hughes turned around in annoyance. "Hey, what's the big idea — *Milo! How's it going?* Great chicken, dude. First-class poultry, no lie!"

I could just make out the top of Kelly Marie's head near the front of the throng. She waved, "Hi, Milo! Come on in! We're feeding Henrietta!"

Milo melted into the teeming crowd. I tried to follow and bounced off Lafayette.

"I'm a close friend of Milo's," I protested.

"In your dreams, nerd!"

It was like the Hollywood parties I'm going to get invited to when I'm a big-time screenwriter. If you're not on the guest list, you're *out*. That dumb pullet was getting to be like a movie star in this school. Only the beautiful people were allowed to hang around.

The only way I got in there at all was when the bell rang and Mrs. Baggio shooed all the tourists away.

Kelly Marie was on her hands and knees in front of the chicken wire. "See, sweetie?" she cooed right into that blank ugly chicken face. "Everybody loves you."

"Because of the hockey team," Adam reminded her.

As usual, Kelly Marie had this all worked out in her warped mind. "I admit that it *was* the Rangers that brought her to public attention. But it was her charm and personality that won everybody over."

"Chickens don't have personality," Milo insisted. "They exist purely —"

"She does so!" countered Kelly Marie. "She's happy and outgoing, but with a quiet, contemplative side —"

"And she's friendly," added Brendan.

"She's great at Monopoly," Sheila put in.

"Oh, come on!" Milo exploded. "The specimen doesn't have anywhere *near* the intelligence necessary to play even the most simple board game!"

"Well, I have to roll for her since her little wings can't

hold the dice," Sheila conceded. "But if she wants to buy a property, she kind of cackles. And when she lands on Free Parking, she gets *really* excited."

This looked like a perfect opportunity to win back a few points with Milo. "No way!" I said with a wink in his direction. "How could a chicken ever put a hotel on Marvin Gardens?"

With a *cheep* of outrage, Henrietta scratched and kicked with her toes, raising up a cloud of sawdust that drifted through the wire and settled on my shoes.

"Hey!" I blurted. "She did that on purpose!"

"Chickens have no purpose, either," Milo said, covering a smirk. Considering he was my best friend, he certainly seemed to enjoy seeing me suffer.

A shriek from Kelly Marie brought the class to attention. She was hopping up and down like a maniac, pointing at the bird's hind end.

"Kelly, what is it?" Mrs. Baggio asked in alarm.

"Look! It's a feather! A *real* feather!"

Big fat hairy deal. The bird had a feather on her butt. But our whole class abandoned their individual projects to rush over and examine this eighth wonder of the world. Whoop-de-doo.

"There's another one!" crowed Brendan, pointing to a wing.

Even Milo kind of got into it, commenting while making notes, "Specimen maturing acceptably."

"Acceptably?!" Kelly Marie was outraged. "Milo Neal, your big brain must be covering your eye sockets! Don't you see what this *really* means? Our little Henrietta is growing up!"

I caught up with Milo again at lunch. But when I sat down beside him, he picked up his tray and moved to another table.

I tried again in gym class, seventh period. Cleverly, I made sure we were on the same vaulting horse. As we flew by in opposite directions, I yelled, "We need to talk!"

But I didn't get to tell him when and where because I got out of sync for our next vault. Coach Crenshaw spotted me trying to sneak ahead in line and sent me to the locker room in disgrace.

Out of the corner of my eye I caught sight of Milo turning his ankle on a tricky landing. In a split-second decision, I smashed my face full-force into the changing room door. The nosebleed was like Niagara Falls.

"Gustafson!" barked the coach, watching my towel turn crimson. "Nurse's office! Now!"

So we were sitting on the bench outside the nurse's office, me bleeding and Milo groaning. I couldn't be sure if he was in agony, because he didn't start making that noise until I sat down beside him.

"How's your leg?" I asked, very nasally.

"You're bleeding on my sneakers," he replied, giving me the worm guts look, complete with sound effects.

I was getting a little annoyed. Didn't he realize that I didn't *have* to have this nosebleed? That I was putting myself through this pain just to get the chance to talk to him?

"Look, Milo, I'm sorry. I didn't mean to abandon your experiment. I had a concussion."

Milo glared at me like no best friend ever should. "That's not what I'm mad about. I'm mad because I phoned to check on the status of the specimen, and you out-and-out lied!"

He had me there. As a total last resort I told the truth. "You and I were just starting to hit it off, and I was afraid this would spoil our friendship. I figured the chicken was probably okay, and maybe I'd never have to tell you."

Milo's expression softened a little. "Yeah, okay, maybe." Then he shook his head in frustration. "But this whole school is nuts! All I'm trying to do here is a science project!"

I shrugged. "And it's going great. The whole school loves Henrietta."

"That's the point!" he exploded. "It's a specimen! It doesn't have anything to do with friendship or hockey or love or popularity! It's a link in the food chain! It exists to be hatched, raised, slaughtered, and eaten! That's my project! Nothing more!"

My ears perked up. "Slaughtered and eaten?"

"What don't you understand?" Milo asked, a little impatiently. "Chickens don't die of old age. They're killed, cooked, and eaten."

I was still in the dark. "Yeah, but you're not going to do *that* part — you know, the killing and the eating?"

"Well, of course I am!" Milo erupted. "What's the point of studying the food chain if we don't complete the link? At the science fair I'm going to serve chicken to the judges while they review the experiment notes."

I goggled. "You mean *our* chicken? Like, *Henrietta* chicken? *Dead* Henrietta chicken?"

"It's the food chain," Milo explained again. "The judges will actually participate in the end of the link. I thought that would be a nice finishing touch."

If Milo had told me that he was an alien and that his nose was about to blast off from his face and burrow down to the earth's core, I wouldn't have been any more surprised. I mean, if Kelly Marie knew this, she'd go supernova. Everybody who had adopted Henrietta as a pet/mascot/hobby/friend — they didn't have the faintest idea that they were looking at an oven-stuffer-in-training! I bet Milo thought it was common knowledge.

That rotten chicken who pecked me, scratched me, and made sure everybody in the world knew how much she hated me — who even gave me a concussion — that fuzzy fiend from the underworld had a date with the frying pan!

I don't get too many moments of ultimate joy, but this was one of them.

Milo interrupted my thoughts. "What are you grinning about?"

"I . . . I think my nose has stopped bleeding."

At that moment, Nurse Jansen appeared, hauled Milo in, and sent out Steve Tenorio with a bandage around his thumb.

The musclehead took one look at my bloody nose and red-stained shirt and grinned nastily. "What happened to you, Zack? Did you get caught in one of your own screenplays?"

But nothing could spoil this perfect day for me. "I'm really happy the Rangers are doing so well with your new mascot," I said, and laughed wildly.

"You're weird!" Steve accused, and walked away.

I was still doubled over when he turned, puzzled, to frown at me.

All week I walked on air, hugging the secret. I got detention for humming. Every time Kelly Marie opened her mouth about Henrietta, I had to leave the room and laugh into my fist in the hall. When I saw all those idiots, who weren't even in our class, lining up to clean chicken droppings from the floor of the pen, the truth was almost bursting out of me: *Don't get too attached to the chicken. She's not staying.*

I went to the hockey pep rally Monday after school.

All the Rangers got a big reception, sure. But then Adam held up Henrietta and the crowd went nuts. A couple of those muscleheads unfurled a banner that said HENRIETTA FOREVER. And I was thinking, Don't count on it.

The Rangers won their fifth in a row, and everyone was talking championship. Oh, I knew what they could serve at the victory banquet!

But seriously — when their good luck charm got sacrificed in the name of science, would Adam and the Rangers start losing again? That would be the icing on the cake — served after a delicious chicken dinner.

When I was in the lab, of course, I played it cool. I didn't want to spill the beans. But every time I looked at that miserable bird I pictured her as a different recipe. Tuesday she was Cajun-style; Wednesday, stuffed and roasted; Thursday, chicken Cordon Bleu; by Friday, I saw fajitas, complete with guacamole and flour tortillas.

Best of all, the end of the week was also the end of Mom's ban on my computer. I'd been so distracted, what with all the happiness and stuff, I hadn't really given a thought to my writer's block and the secret identity of the brain-eating psycho-monster. But I was confident. It wasn't even Saturday yet, and as I drifted off into sleep, *The Brain Eaters* was playing itself out like a movie in my half-dreams.

I saw the psycho-monster stalking through the streets and stopping in front of the university lab. Its hideous features began to distort as it mutated into its secret identity — a form so innocent and harmless that it could move among its victims without creating a stampede of terror. Then, in a split second, it could crack open a dozen heads and be popping down brains like peanuts.

I was just about asleep, but I struggled to stay awake enough to see the end of the mutation — the secret identity. The psycho-monster's new features coalesced and came into focus. The homicidal, archevildoer was now — a big chicken!

I sat bolt upright in bed. *A chicken?!*

Fade to black . . .

9 🐔

FROM THE DIARY OF MRS. BAGGIO

I must confess that I'm beginning to feel a little uneasy about the chicken project. I suppose I should have seen it coming. But I was so overwhelmed by the thought of *teaching* Victor Neal's son that I fear I missed the big picture: I'm barely tolerated at this school; Henrietta is the object of worship.

Oh, this is nothing new. Put a hamster or a rabbit in a classroom and you have an instant fan club. The students will do anything for a warm-blooded creature that nibbles. And with Henrietta — well, perhaps it was the novelty of a chicken, mixed with the fame of Milo and his father. And now this strange hockey connection. It was spontaneous combustion, an overnight success story. A star was born.

I've never had so many students come into my lab;

I've never seen so much interest in science. All books on chickens have been checked out of the school library. Students discuss the nutritional value of birdseed when they used to talk about rock and roll. Volunteers waiting their turn with Henrietta now play my Quizzles and my math games. My gyroscope is spinning again. One hockey player who can barely remember his times tables has me tutoring him on calculating trajectory and acceleration to improve his slap shot. All because Henrietta has brought them to my room. It's a science teacher's dream. Except —

Henrietta will be dead in a few weeks. Milo's project calls for it.

I circulated among my students to make sure they were okay with that.

"It's a fact of life," I told Sheila Martel. "All chickens are raised to be eaten."

"Yeah," she agreed. "Thank God that isn't going to happen with Henrietta."

I raised the same topic with Joey Sorrentino and Lynette Martinez. They both looked one hundred percent blank.

"Chickens are food!" I persisted. "Where do you think *chicken* comes from? They don't carve it off a warthog, you know!"

"But Henrietta's a *school* chicken." Joey lectured me like I needed to be straightened out on the subject. "*Farm* chickens are the ones that you eat."

With Kelly Marie, I just said it right out: "When a chicken gets big enough, you slaughter it and eat it."

She looked me straight in the eye. "If anybody tried that with Henrietta, I'd break every bone in his body!"

I had to face the facts. No one had the slightest idea what was coming at the end of Milo's project. Furthermore, when that information got out, I was going to have a riot on my hands.

Oh, what a pickle!

I even went so far as to approach Milo. "Perhaps it might be nice to have Henrietta in a cage on display at the science fair," I suggested brightly. "Then you could serve Real Dixie Fried Chicken to *symbolize* her place in the food chain."

He was horrified. "That negates my whole experiment! How can I make my specimen an exception to the food chain when the whole purpose is to show that there *are* no exceptions to the food chain?"

And he was right, of course. Besides, I'm the one who invested so much of my own and the class's time in Milo's project. To make him change it would not only be unfair — it would make *me* look like a proper fool.

So I'm caught between a rock and a hard place. What can I do? Oh, dear, what *can* I do?

10

FROM THE SUPER·SECRET
RECORDINGS OF JOEY SORRENTINO

Lynette says it was fate that the Neals got divorced, and
Milo and his mom moved to St. Martin, and Milo ended
up going to our school. Lynette says it was no accident
that Milo got put in the Bag's class, and that he was
doing his project on a chicken, and that chicken turned
out to be Henrietta. It was destiny. That's what Lynette
says.

Me? I agree with her, mostly because disagreeing
with Lynette is bad business. The last time I disagreed
with her, we broke up. And the time before that. And
the time before *that*. But enough of my love life. This is
supposed to be about Henrietta.

She's the greatest. Our dog is lazy and he has bad
breath, and I'm positive our cat has a split personality.

My brother's hamster is a near-idiot, running on that dumb wheel all day. But when I look into Henrietta's bright chicken eyes, I know I've got a friend who'll never let me down. Lynette says Henrietta and I are on the same wavelength, although I'm pretty sure I heard somewhere that chickens can't swim.

Take last night's Ranger game for example. We were down 6–3 against Minnetonka, and Steve was still out with his sprained thumb, and Adam was in the penalty box for a misconduct, and the Wall was even worse than usual in net, and DeeVee was benched because he took a crazy slap shot and busted the skylight in the Community Center. Our fans were leaving, and Coach Crenshaw was yelling, and the winning streak was going down the tubes.

Then all of a sudden, Henrietta squawked. Not any little baby chirp, but a real grown-up chicken squawk, her first one.

"Time out!" bellowed a voice.

"Time out?" echoed the coach in disbelief. "Only I call time out! Who said that?"

It was Kelly Marie, who always sat directly behind the team so she could keep an eye on Henrietta.

"Did you hear that?" She climbed out of her seat and onto our bench, and picked up the old parrot cage that was Henrietta's home during Ranger games. "She squawked! And she ruffled her little feathers! I saw!"

"What's wrong with the chicken?" called Adam anxiously from the penalty box.

"She squawked!" called half a dozen Rangers in a state of high excitement.

"She's trying to tell us something!" I said breathlessly. "She sees how lousy we've been playing!"

"You don't need a chicken to tell you that!" Coach Crenshaw was starting to look a little upset.

"You guys make me sick!" Kelly Marie snorted. "You don't care about Henrietta as a person! You're not interested that she's growing up! You just want her to help you play stupid hockey!"

The coach blew his stack. "What's so bad about that? We're a hockey *team!* This is a hockey *rink!* We're in the middle of a hockey *game!* What are we supposed to play — *Yahtzee?!*"

The referee skated over. "Rangers, your time's up."

"But Henrietta talked," DeeVee explained, "and we can't figure out what she said."

"I'll tell you what she said!" roared the ref. "She said get your butts on the ice or you're getting a penalty for delay of game! That's what she said!"

Then Henrietta squawked again and, from that moment on, our feet had wings. We scored five goals in five minutes to win the game 8–6. An amazing come-from-behind victory — and we owed it all to our mascot.

Lynette says Henrietta squawked to show that, just

like *she* was maturing, *we* had to mature as a hockey team. Man, I'd like to see any dog or cat do that.

Thanks to Henrietta, November was shaping up to be the greatest month in my life. The Rangers were the hottest middle-school team in Minnesota, and after Adam, I was the top scorer. We had won eight straight since our 0 and 5 start, and we'd already broken the top ten in our division.

Lynette says it's not hard to feel good when everything's going your way. I agree with that, and it's not even because I'm afraid she'll break up with me again. In fact, Lynette and I have been getting along so well that it's almost scary. We haven't gotten into a real screaming fight since the day before yesterday. And even then we only broke up for half an hour or so. It's Henrietta. I swear it.

Here's why. When we got to school every morning, Lynette used to get really cheesed at me because I'd blow her off and go play tennis-ball hockey with Adam, Laffy, and Steve. But now the two of us head straight for the lab to see if the Bag needs any help with Henrietta. This alone avoids at least two breakups a week.

Not only that, but it used to drive her nuts that I'd pick the raisins out of my cinnamon bun at lunch every day. Now she knows I slip them to Henrietta, so it's okay. And she can't complain that we don't talk enough.

We spend hours and hours discussing chickens, reading about chickens, and making ourselves ready for the big day: After weeks of anticipation, our names had finally made it to the top of the waiting list. Milo was going to let us take Henrietta home for the weekend. And we had special plans.

Lynette says it's going to be historic.

11 🐤

EXPERIMENT NOTES: MILO NEAL
11/22

> It's not so bad coming home from school Monday through Thursday. I've got homework to do and experiment notes to update. Before you know it, it's time to go to sleep so I can start the process over tomorrow.

> But on Friday, my excuses for being busy are gone. That's when Mom shifts into high gear:

"You should get out more. You're not sociable. You need to be with people your own age. You never see a living soul all weekend."

{This never happened in California, although I was usually by myself there, too. Perhaps it = worry re: new town & school/further study req'd.}

"Why don't you get together with your friend

Zachary?" she would suggest over and over. "Or how about that girl who came by? What was her name?"

"Kelly Marie."

"She left you her number. Give her a call."

"They're both weird." That was my standard answer.

> The problem might have been a little easier if I had my specimen to care for over Saturday and Sunday. But thanks to Mrs. B, that was never going to happen. {Why is it such a big deal to "help" me by taking the subj. for the weekend? Joey S and Lynette M practically danced with the cage all the way out of the lab. And it's not just those two. There are thirty-one names on the sign-up sheet — baffling because the experiment will be over long before thirty-one weeks, and subj. will no longer exist/further study req'd.}

> But when I got home that Friday, my mother wasn't in nagging mode at all. In fact, she was waiting by the door, beaming.

"I have the most wonderful news!" she said.

I brightened. "Dad's coming?"

She gave me a sympathetic smile. "No, Milo. Not yet. But guess what? You've been invited to a party tonight!"

I stared at her. "By who?"

"I've got all the information on the telephone pad upstairs. What a nice girl — so friendly. She really sounded excited about having you come."

"Aw, Mom," I groaned, "you know I hate parties."

"How can you say that if you never go to any?" she demanded.

> I never stick my head in the furnace, either, but I know it's lousy.

"I'm not going," I insisted. "I won't know anybody there."

"That's not true!" my mother pounced on it. "The girl having the party must know you, right? Otherwise why would she call to invite you?"

"Because my chicken is more popular than Santa Claus," I explained bitingly, "and definitely a whole lot more popular than me."

"Well, Zachary's going to be at the party," she countered.

> This is why my mother should never go into sales. ZG is not going to put me over the top re: this party. This = a real estate agent saying, "Buy this house — it's built on a nice toxic waste dump."

I said, "How could you know that Zachary will be there?"

She looked a little sheepish. "I phoned him. He says he'll meet you at the party."

"That'll be a trick because I'm not going."

Suddenly, Mom changed tactics and decided to play it cool. "Okay. I certainly can't force you to go if you don't want to, even though you'll be miserable staying around here."

> She personally would be supplying the misery.

"Fine."

"Now, you go and lie around the house like a sack of flour, and I'll call you when dinner's ready."

> I had to admire her willpower. I knew she was dying to run upstairs to get her message pad so she could read me the details of this party. I admit I was a little curious myself. Who was the mysterious hostess? But I would have died before asking.

> The standoff stayed friendly through dinner. Then, while I was loading the dishwasher, I noticed Mom's speech had become short and clipped. Later, in front of the TV, the silent treatment began. But I could see her glancing toward the stairs, which led up to the details of the party I hoped I was missing by now.

{My mother looks totally serene when she's angry. But you can almost hear the hiss of the boiler room filling up with steam just below the surface/further study req'd.}

Finally, I could take it no longer. *"What?"*

She glared at me. "I can accept that you don't want to go to this party. But the least you can do is phone that poor girl and tell her you can't make it."

"Oh, all right," I sighed. "What's the number?"

> She dashed upstairs and returned seconds later with a sheet from her memo pad. I stared.

Lynette Martinez

18 Apple Blossom Lane

7:30 P.M.

I was shocked. "That's impossible!"

"I took the message myself, Milo."

"But Lynette can't be having a party!" I protested. "She's looking after my specimen this weekend!"

It was my mother's turn to sigh. "You and your father — honestly! The world has to grind to a halt for the experiment! Do you really think this Lynette might endanger your chicken?"

> I imagined the kind of party LM might have. I didn't conjure up the image of people in tuxedos playing Parcheesi while a string quartet performed Mozart.

I ran for my coat. "I've got to get over there!"

A wide grin split my mother's face. "Don't forget to bring money. You might have to chip in for the pizza or something."

"I'm not going as a guest!" I roared.

"I should have known," she laughed. "You're going as a killjoy. That'll do wonders for your social life."

"I've got to retrieve my specimen!"

> But I knew Mom was right. In addition to a nerd, a brain, an outsider, and a conceited snob, I was now going to be known as a party pooper.

> Why me?/further study req'd.

12

RANGERS UPDATE:
CAPTAIN ADAM LURIE REPORTING

Leave it to Joey and Lynette to throw a party in honor of a chicken.

That's what they called it — a Henrietta Appreciation Bash. Don't get me wrong. I appreciated Henrietta just fine. I mean, we hadn't lost a game yet with her sitting on our bench. But I love her the way you'd love any good luck charm that was working for you — like a rabbit's foot or a horseshoe. This was like throwing a Presidential Gala for a four-leaf clover.

But you didn't pass up a chance to go to one of Lynette's parties. For starters, she had the loudest stereo in St. Martin and the perfect place to put it. The Martinez house had a giant attic converted into a rec room. Strip hardwood made the ultimate dance floor and the place was filled with beanbag chairs. They had the works — video games, a wide-screen TV, air hockey, a pinball machine, and, across a corner by the window, the coolest, most comfortable hammock in the world.

Mr. and Mrs. Martinez had gone into Minneapolis for a wedding, and Lynette had gotten their permission to "have a few friends over." There were forty-five people in the attic when I got there and everyone was in a big-party mood. The dancing had just gotten under way, although the floor wasn't that crowded yet. A lot of the kids were over at the food table, helping themselves to snacks, ice cream, and a mountain of nachos at least three feet high.

The best thing about Lynette's parties was that they were a great place to be seen, especially for a hockey player like me. Lynette and Joey hung out with the cool people — the Rangers, the cheerleaders, mostly eighth-graders, and even a few freshmen from the high school. I was really impressed to see Tony Walters, Brendan's older brother, the *real* Wall. I wish we still had him in goal. Brendan was a nice guy, and he tried really hard, but just seeing Tony brought back memories of last year. The Wall was our MVP and the league's shutout king. He led us to a season of 12–3–2 *and* the championship before the Canadians skunked us 11–zip at Christmas.

Henrietta sat in her cage on that awesome hammock in the corner, watching the goings-on with unruffled calm. It didn't seem to bother her that Laffy, playing DJ,

was cranking the music louder with every song. She
wasn't alarmed in the slightest that the attic was filling
up to capacity and the floor was shaking with the vibra-
tions of so many dancing feet. There was a real cool attitude to this chicken; either that or she was too dumb
to notice the joint was jumping.

Just when it seemed like everything was about to hit
fever pitch, suddenly Lafayette pulled the plug on the
stereo, and Joey and Lynette managed to get the place
quieted down.

"Attention, everybody," called Lynette. "We'll get
back to the music and the fun, but let's take a few minutes to salute our guest of honor, Henrietta."

Joey lifted the cage from the hammock and held it
high. There was a big cheer.

I picked up a couple of wisecracks from the ninth-
graders. But when they saw how seriously the rest of us
were taking this, they shut right up.

Then Steve and DeeVee and a couple of the cheerleaders circulated through the crowd with large bottles
of diet soda, filling up everybody's glasses.

Our hostess raised her drink. "To Henrietta!" she
cried in ringing tones. "Mascot . . . chicken . . . friend."

As we all stood there with our glasses held high,
Laffy cued the music:

. . . I can fly higher than an eagle!
You are the wind beneath my wings.

I don't think it's disloyal to the Rangers to admit that I'd never felt so stupid in my life. Picture it — sixty people standing around toasting a chicken while the music blared about flying eagles. At least nobody could make fun of me, because everybody I knew was right there, doing the same idiotic thing.

Fortunately, it was over fast. Laffy cut to some decent rock and roll, and there was a stampede for the dance floor.

Joey and Lynette waded into the gyrating crowd, holding Henrietta's cage high between them.

I made a bolt for the hammock in the corner, but Steve got there a split second ahead of me. I grabbed the fabric at two strategic points and flipped, sending him tumbling to the floor. In a flash, I was in the hammock, luxuriating in the perfect comfort.

My joy lasted about three seconds. For there, pushing his way through the crowd in front of the nachos, was none other than Zachary Gustafson. I stared, unable to believe my own eyes. The one thing I thought you could depend on at Lynette's parties was that you would never run into any losers, let alone the world champion checkered-flag speed demon of the Loserapolis 500!

I launched myself out of the hammock, grabbed the party-crashing dweeb, and steered him away from the roaring floor-to-ceiling speakers. "Are you crazy, Zack? What are you doing here?"

Dweeb-asaurus played Mr. Innocent. "I was invited."
I stared him down. "Well, not really," he admitted.
"But my good friend Milo was, and I'm meeting him."

"Milo . . . ?" But then I realized that of course
Henrietta's owner would have to make the guest list.
Otherwise Lynette would never invite a sixth-grader,
aside from Brendan, who was a Ranger.

"Okay, meet Milo," I said grudgingly. "But the hammock is off-limits." Some things had to stay sacred.

I could tell Zachary was pretty impressed by his sur-
roundings. After all, how many chances would a loser
like him have to get in on the kind of party Lynette
throws? And I have to say that it was getting consider-
ably awesome.

People were arriving in a steady stream, and the attic
was jam-packed. You could tell that word of the party
had spread around town, because there were a lot of
people there who definitely weren't from South Middle
School. Some of them looked like high school students — even juniors and seniors. A few looked like ex-
traterrestrials, with nose rings, dog collars, and blue
hair. The place was so steamy from all those bodies that
even with the window wide open I was sweating. Laffy
had the stereo up to nine by now, with the bass maxed
out. You could feel each drumbeat in your kidneys.
There were so many kids on the dance floor that they
were belly to belly, bumping and gyrating, a single
seething mass. All arms were raised and Henrietta's

cage was being rolled from hand to hand above the dancers.

Barbara Falconi grabbed me by the arm and hauled me out onto the floor, which was a pretty tight squeeze. Suddenly, Henrietta's cage bounced off my head. I looked up and caught a brief glimpse of our upside-down mascot pressed against the bars. I don't claim to be a professor of tweety-birds, but her eyes were bulging, and her neck was drawn back into her feathers — she sure didn't look very happy to me.

I grabbed the back of Joey's collar and turned him around to face me. "Maybe we should give her a rest!" I shouted, pointing at the cage.

"You're right!" he bellowed back. "She *is* the best!"

So much for trying to be heard.

Then I was distracted by a pretty hilarious sight — Milo Neal trying to push his way across the dance floor. He looked like a guy wading through a neck-deep river of molasses. Dancing bodies bumped him, and flailing arms smacked him about the head. But his face was a study of anger and effort, and he forged on. He kept repeating something over and over. Even though I couldn't hear him above the ruckus, I knew what he was saying:

"Where's my specimen?!"

As much as I was enjoying seeing the crown prince of California science in such a panic, I reached up for the cage so I could show it to Milo. After a minute, I felt the metal bars against my hand. I latched onto the cage and pulled it down. But even before I saw it, I knew it felt too light. I stared in horror. The little gate was open and Henrietta was gone.

But California Boy wasn't looking at the cage at all. His horrified eyes were fixed on Tony Walters — the Wall — on the other side of the dance floor. Tony moved to the beat, both arms straight up over his head. His fingertips gripped a familiar bundle of feathers.

I shouted, *"Wa-a-all!"*

But it was too late. The frightened chicken wriggled herself free and began scrambling across dancers' heads, deftly leaping over the sea of grabbing hands. It was amazing — eighty of us and only one of her, and she made it, flapping and scratching. She hopped across us like we were stepping stones, scooted up the slope of the hammock, and disappeared out the open window.

There was a collective gasp that almost ate up all the oxygen in the room. Laffy cut the music and joined the stampede to the window.

Milo and I got there first. We looked down, fully expecting to see a heap of broken feathers on the grass three floors below us. But there was nothing there.

"Did she bounce?" I asked weakly, picturing our hockey season as dead as Henrietta probably now was.

Then we heard that squawk and it wasn't coming from the ground. We looked up and there she was, perched on a branch of the big apple tree in the Martinezes' yard.

"Fascinating," said Milo. "Her wings managed to take her the eighteen inches from the ledge to the nearest branch. The specimen is maturing rapidly."

Lynette and Joey pushed their way to our side.

"Henrietta!" Lynette shrieked out into the night. "You come back here this minute!"

In answer, the bird backed away a few steps on the branch.

Zachary rushed forward — like we needed him! "I've got an idea, Milo!" he babbled. "You hold onto my ankles, and I'll hang out the window and grab the branch, forming a human bridge. Henrietta can just walk across me right back into the house!"

In the golden age of stupid ideas, that one will still be a classic. "Don't tempt me, Zack," I muttered. "If you're going out that window, you're going all the way."

Milo started for the stairs. "Someone get a ladder," he ordered briskly. "The specimen is too frightened to come in on her own. I'll have to go up and get her."

I'm not a big Milo fan, but I had to be impressed by the way this L.A. kid took charge. I mean, Lynette was in tears, Joey was paralyzed with guilt, the high-schoolers were still fooling around, and the rest of us were as useful as a flock of sheep aboard the starship *Enterprise*.

In a body, we all followed Milo down the stairs and

out into the yard. We gathered around the base of the apple tree, peering up into the branches. In the gloom, it was hard to pick out Henrietta.

Zachary spotted her first. "There she is!"

High above us, the tweety-bird shifted on her branch, dislodging an old, frozen, wormy apple. It dropped like a bomb, catching Zachary full in the mush.

"Ow!"

Lynette came running from around the front.

"Where's the ladder?" asked Milo.

"We don't have one!" she wailed. "So I called 911!"

I listened. You could already hear the sirens in the distance.

Well, the high school guys — they thought that was just great. To them this was the icing on the cake — you had a wild party, and you topped it off with a police raid. They started horsing around on the lawn, laughing and shouting and hurling clumps of frozen turf at each other.

"Cut it out, you guys!" shrieked Lynette. "This is serious! Henrietta's in danger! Joey, make them stop!"

"Come on, everybody! Chill out!" Joey pleaded.

The roughhousing raged on. I doubt the high-schoolers even heard him. They did calm down a little to watch the fire truck roar up the Martinezes' driveway. Four rubber-coated firefighters leaped down and squeaked over in their humongous boots.

Lynette ran screaming over to meet them. "Henrietta's in a tree and we can't get her down!"

"Don't worry, miss." The fire chief trained his high-powered flashlight up into the branches of the apple tree. It illuminated our mascot, perched on the flimsy branch, terrified and shivering from the cold.

"I don't see her," said the chief.

"Right there!" yelled a dozen of us, pointing. Even the high-schoolers were starting to get involved.

The chief squinted. "Did she climb up there to rescue the chicken?"

"She *is* the chicken!" bawled Lynette.

The man stared. "You called 911 for a *chicken?*"

I stepped forward. "I know it sounds stupid, but she's our mascot!"

"And she's the wind beneath our wings!" chimed in DeeVee.

"She's a link in the food chain," Milo corrected severely.

"She's everybody's friend!" quavered Lynette. "Please, please, *please* get her down!"

The chief scratched his head. "Well, I suppose we can't just leave her there."

So they dragged out the ladder and hauled Henrietta down from the tree. But they sure didn't look too happy about it. I guess we should be grateful they didn't turn the hose on us.

"Quick, get a blanket," ordered Milo. "The specimen shouldn't be exposed to this kind of cold."

"Here." Joey pulled his sweater over his head and wrapped it around the bird in Milo's arms.

Lynette was trembling with emotion. "I'm never going to forgive you for this, Joey! This is all your fault!"

"*My* fault?" Joey repeated. "It was *your* party!"

"But it was *your* idea!"

"Which I got from *you!*"

In a rage, Lynette tore his signet ring from her finger and bounced it with deadly accuracy off his forehead.

"We're finished!" they chorused in perfect unison and ran off in opposite directions.

I stepped up and put a sympathetic arm around Milo's shoulders. "Look, Milo, we're sorry —"

Stiffly, he shook me off, wheeled, and stalked away, taking his chicken home.

Zachary ran after him, waving the empty cage. "Wait up, Milo, buddy! I'm coming!"

13

"PSYCHOLOGY TALK"
BY KELLY MARIE GINSBERG

Weekend mornings were newspaper mornings at my house. We got the *Minneapolis Tribune* on Sunday, but Saturdays were reserved for the *St. Martin Sentinel,* our local weekly. My dad had the sports and Mom was reading the editorials. I poured myself some orange juice and sat down with the front section.

The *Sentinel* was more of a family tradition than a really good paper because not much ever happened in our sleepy little city. I breezed quickly through the headlines — nothing interesting, as usual, until one word popped off the page at me: CHICKEN.

TEENS CALL 911 TO RESCUE CHICKEN AFTER WILD PARTY

My blood froze. I read on, hoping against hope that the article was about some other chicken.

> A teen party got out of hand last night, and a defenseless animal nearly paid the price. The fire department was called to 18 Apple Blossom Lane to rescue someone named Henrietta only to discover that Henrietta was not a person but a chicken belonging to Milo Neal, son of the famous Victor Neal. The chicken, which figures in young Neal's science project, became frightened when the party grew rowdy and fled via an attic window, marooning herself in a tall apple tree . . .

I dropped the paper as though it burned my fingers. *"Those stupid brainless morons!"*

My mother jumped. "What is it, dear?"

I showed her the article. "And I know who did it, too — Joey and Lynette! *They* had Henrietta this weekend! And that's Lynette's address!"

Dad read over Mom's shoulder. "I remember when we used to do stuff like this back at the frat house," he chuckled. "It's all in fun."

"It wasn't much fun for Henrietta!" I seethed. "Poor little sweetie! She could have been lost or even killed!

Not to mention that she was running loose in a party full of crazy people! She could have been stomped on!"

"Now, Kelly," my mother warned, "I hope you're not planning to do anything rash."

I was already lacing my second sneaker. "I'm going to take Henrietta away from those incompetent low-grade nitwits!"

I knocked on the door of 18 Apple Blossom Lane. The lady who answered looked a lot like Lynette, so I assumed she was Mrs. Martinez.

"Hi," I greeted. "Is Lynette here?"

Mrs. Martinez's brow clouded. "Lynette is grounded for the week. And if you were at that awful party last night, you should be grounded, too."

"Oh, I wasn't even invited," I defended myself. I noted that she was wearing sweats and holding a huge green garbage bag. Obviously, the cleanup from last night was a major operation. "What I really wanted to know . . . uh . . . is Henrietta still here?"

Mrs. Martinez frowned. "I told you — Lynette isn't seeing any of her friends for at least a week." She glanced at the garbage bag. "Maybe two."

"No, no. I mean Henrietta — the chicken."

Mrs. Martinez's mouth dropped open. "There was a *chicken?*" She recovered a little. "Well, I suppose that would explain the feathers and . . . uh . . . other things we found in the rec room."

I thanked her and left, heading double-speed for the only other place Henrietta could be — Milo's house.

Mrs. Neal let me in. "We've been expecting you, Kelly Marie," she beamed, throwing the door wide and ushering me in as though I were visiting royalty.

I stared at her. "How did you know I was coming?"

But then I caught sight of the living room. Draped in various poses around the comfortable furniture were Milo, Zachary, Adam, and Joey.

"Hi," said Adam weakly.

I swooped down like an avenging angel. "Don't *hi* me! I could kill you guys! Twice! Where's Henrietta?"

"In the kitchen with the vet," said Milo. "I think she has a fever."

I looked daggers at Joey. "You and your wacko girlfriend couldn't leave well enough alone!"

"She's not my girlfriend anymore," said Joey, tight-lipped.

I snorted with disgust. "Don't worry. You and Lynette are getting married. Why ruin two houses?"

Zachary spoke up. "How did you know there was a party?"

"The whole town knows! You idiots made the paper! Mrs. Baggio's probably reading all about it right now!"

"She already phoned," said Milo mournfully.

Mrs. Neal appeared carrying a tray loaded with bagels and muffins and steaming mugs of hot chocolate.

"I'm so thrilled that you all came over today," she smiled, setting everything out on the coffee table.

I cocked an eyebrow. Mrs. Neal must have been pretty worried about her son not having any friends. Here we were, in a sickbed vigil for Henrietta, and Milo's mother was acting like this was a tea party.

The guys fell on the food like ravenous tigers. I sipped a bit of chocolate. "You must be *really* broken up over Henrietta," I said sarcastically. "Your appetites are suffering."

"It's not going to help the specimen if we starve," offered Zachary.

"Oh, you too with 'the specimen,'" I exclaimed. "If you sit too close to Milo, he rubs off on you?"

We all rose as Dr. Siltinen, the veterinarian, appeared in the doorway, holding Henrietta wrapped in a wool blanket.

"Well, Milo, you have a pretty sick bird here."

I heard Joey gulp. "Is she going to . . . you know, *die?*"

"She's suffered a severe chill," the vet replied. "I'm prescribing antibiotics to prevent it from turning into pneumonia. If you keep her warm and quiet, she should be back to normal in a few days."

I heaved a tremulous sigh. "Oh, thank you Dr. Siltinen! You're the greatest —"

But Adam Hockey-Is-My-Life Lurie had to open his

mouth and prove what a low-down two-faced selfish pig he is. "But we've got a game on Monday! She can come to the rink, right?"

"Absolutely not," said the vet firmly. "Cold, damp air is exactly what you have to avoid."

Adam was in agony. "It's not that cold! We'll wrap her up! She'll have a hot water bottle! We'll get a heater! Oh, please —"

With all my might, I stomped on his foot. It shut him up in a flash. If he'd opened his mouth, a shriek would have come out.

"No." The doctor was adamant. "The chicken is not to leave the house for the next seventy-two hours."

"We're playing Mount Carmel," Joey said hopefully. "They're the worst team in the state. Maybe we can beat them without Henrietta."

Henrietta squawked, not her usual perky, energetic sound, but a weak, pitiful mewl. My heart broke in two. So I began a long lecture, heavy on the psychology, about what was wrong with each and every one of those insects —.and what would happen to them if they ever mistreated Henrietta again.

14

DOWNLOADED FROM THE FILES OF ZACHARY GUSTAFSON

WE MEET AT LAST

[Scene 56]

[EXTERIOR SHOT: The White House – day]

Finally, the moment has arrived — our first ever contact with an alien race. The galactic spacecraft, which looks a little small, sets down on the White House landing pad.

PRESIDENT ZOT

Citizens of the world, today we get our first glimpse of life forms from outside the Milky Way galaxy . . .

Instead of opening, the spaceship door disintegrates, an example of the highly advanced technology of the

space travelers. The Marine band strikes up a welcoming march. The CAPTAIN emerges with his crew — interstellar chickens —

Chickens?!

I pulled back from the computer in disbelief. Why
did I type that? I didn't *plan* for the interstellar visitors to
be chickens. That's one of the problems of being a true
natural writer. The story comes from your gut, not your
brain. Why did my gut want *chickens* to be in *We Meet
at Last?* I don't even like chickens. I only knew one, and
she would be dead long before the gala Hollywood
opening for *We Meet at Last.* First *The Brain Eaters* and
now this! Why were all these chickens invading my
screenplays?

To get my mind off my writing problems, I spent a lot
of time at Milo's place that weekend. Officially I was visiting the sick chicken. It was the perfect excuse to work
on Milo a little more.

Unfortunately, the whole world had the same idea.
The house was like Epcot Center. It was packed!

Kelly Marie practically lived there, fussing over
Henrietta. There were also a lot of hockey players in
and out, visiting their mascot and scarfing down the
endless trays of snacks Mrs. Neal put out. Not to mention the constant *boom! . . . boom! . . . boom!* of DeeVee
outside on the driveway, practicing his slap shot against
the aluminum garage door.

Being around so many Rangers was dangerous for a guy like me, but I took the heat to spend so much time with Milo.

"Dweeb . . . geek . . . suck-up . . . loser . . ."

Nobody actually said it out loud; the words just kind of bubbled up from the background every time I managed to sidle up to the man of the house.

Naturally, Kelly Marie had to stick her nose into it. "This is textbook psychology," she explained to the team. "Zachary represents all your hidden insecurities."

"What a load of garbage," Adam groaned.

Suddenly, Lafayette bounded in through the sliding door and stuffed a mittful of snow down my shirt.

"*Yeeeow!*" I jumped up and down, brushing it out.

"The carpet! The carpet!" warned Milo, giving me the worm guts look. Like I was manufacturing the snow in my belly button.

"See?" Kelly Marie was triumphant. "When you pick on Zachary, you're really picking on yourselves."

"So how come I'm the one with the f-f-frozen stomach?" I muttered, teeth chattering.

"In psychology it's the same thing," she said smugly, and launched into one of her famous lectures.

She got the hockey players so riled that Steve grabbed me by the belt, and Lafayette gave me a killer wedgie.

"Aw, come on!" I complained, my legs dangling as they held me up. I pointed at Kelly Marie. "*She's* the one you're mad at!"

"Yeah," Steve explained as the two muscleheads carried me out to the backyard, "but you're not allowed to wedgie a girl."

"Sure you are!" I exploded. "Girls can be firefighters and senators and astronauts! They can get wedgies, too!"

As usual, my protests fell on deaf ears. They wrapped the back of my underwear over a fence post and hung me there, struggling and freezing. Through the frosted windows I could make out Kelly Marie — toasty warm — still raving about psychology.

Milo was the one who got me down. I was really impressed by the fact that he saw me hanging for only about five minutes before coming to rescue me.

I decided to play up the friendship angle. "Thanks, pal," I said when I was on the ground again. "You sure came through for me there!"

Milo looked stricken. "I just can't believe *any* of this!"

"I know," I sympathized. "Who would've thought a chicken could get so sick?"

"Not *that!*" he cried. "I mean, why is everybody *here?* The experiment suffered a setback and I'm dealing with it. That's all."

I shrugged. "I guess they're worried about Henrietta."

"Worry has no medical value!" raged Milo. "Kelly Marie has taken over my house! Joey has red eyes from pining over Lynette and my specimen! My mother just sent him up to take a nap in *my* bed! The hockey team is eating us out of house and home! How is *that* supposed to help a sick chicken?"

Secretly, I was celebrating. Milo *never* opened up like this to anybody. It probably meant we were turning into really close friends. I manufactured a sigh of shared suffering. "These guys, they just don't understand the science way like we do."

In my mind, we weren't freezing in Milo's yard. We were sipping coconut frostees at Victor Neal's pool while Mel Gibson begged me to let him play President Zot. With stuff like that to look forward to, what's a wedgie here and there?

In the meantime, I planned to take my revenge in little ways. On Monday, the Rangers had to play without Henrietta. If they stank, it meant they were going straight down the drain the instant Milo put his project into the final phase.

And I intended to be there — in the front row with my dad's trumpet — to root big-time, heart and soul, rah! rah! for the other team.

Fade to black . . .

15

RANGERS UPDATE:
CAPTAIN ADAM LURIE REPORTING

Okay, I admit it wasn't Zachary's fault that we couldn't beat the worst team in the league. We had nobody to blame but ourselves that we wound up in a 5–5 tie with Mount Carmel, the state joke since Coach Crenshaw was a Ranger.

Fine. We played lousy. For some crazy reason we were useless without our mascot. But to suffer the added humiliation of one of our own South Middle School students cheering for Mount Carmel — that loser — worse, the number one expert Professor of Loserology at Loser U — it was too much! It was the end!

So I arrived at school on Tuesday with a mission — Dweebicide. Zachary was a dead loser. Then I was

going to find Milo and tell him that Henrietta was coming to our next game even if she was in the final stages
of bubonic plague. I didn't care if she was on a stretcher
with a breathing tube in her beak and an IV sticking out
of her wing. The Rangers weren't setting blade to ice
without our chicken.

I found Zachary at a cafeteria table, poring over one
of his stupid screenplays. It would have been smart to
sneak up on the little Benedict Loser, but I was so mad
I just blurted out, "You're dead, man!"

He grabbed the script and bolted. I must say that, for
a loser, he was pretty fast. But no sixth-grader was going
to outrun a varsity athlete, and I had payback on my
mind.

"Heads up!" I called, hurdling some eighth-graders
who were working on a big poster. My foot cleared the
tall girl's head by a quarter of an inch. I hit the floor running and did a quick spin-o-rama around the band
teacher, who was carrying a tuba under each arm. It
slowed me down a little, but I still caught sight of
Zachary disappearing into the far stairwell. That meant
he was probably heading for science class.

I flew down the stairs three at a time and pelted into
the lab. There I saw exactly what I expected to see —
Zachary doing the Gustafson Shuffle right behind Mrs.
Baggio. I was breathing hard and seeing red. My eyes
must have been bulging out of my head.

"Adam —" The Bag turned to me angrily. I was nailed for sure when Kelly Marie's voice rose above the general hum:

"Look! It's Henrietta!"

I wheeled. There was Milo, carrying that beautiful, adorable, *essential* chicken!

"She's okay again?" I asked as the class burst into cheers and applause.

"Dr. Siltinen said the specimen has made a one hundred percent recovery," Milo announced. "I've weighed her and considering the —"

"Hello, sweetie!" shrieked Kelly Marie, making an end run and yanking the cage from Milo's hands. "Everybody missed you *so much!* You look *wonderful!*"

I figured I'd better get it spelled out. "I mean, she's okay to come to the rink, right?"

"If you're *very* careful with her," Milo said grudgingly.

Henrietta squawked and the whole class crowded around her.

"Look how much she's grown!"

"She's smiling! She's happy to be back!"

"See, Henrietta? I'm wearing your favorite shirt!"

"Look how many new feathers she's got!"

Even the Bag joined the admiration society. She and Kelly Marie placed the chicken back in the pen amidst the get-well cards from almost every homeroom in the school. The class stood around like proud parents as Henrietta began poking and prodding the cards with her beak and taking the occasional bite out of the daisies Lynette had brought over.

That was when I made my move. I cornered Zachary behind the Mars globe and lifted him up by his collar. "Well, Loser, I hear you're a big hockey fan — for Mount Carmel Junior High!"

Naturally, the dweeb tried to weasel out of it. "It wasn't me! It was somebody else!"

"If you wanted to keep a low profile," I growled, "you should have left the trumpet at home!"

"You've got me all wrong!" Zachary blubbered. "I was *for* you guys! Go Rangers!"

"Well, it's too bad you won't be able to cheer us on anymore," I snarled. "If I see your ugly face within a mile of the rink, the whole team's going to skate over your neck!"

The dweeb flushed with anger. "Who wants to see your crummy old team?"

I lifted him up another foot and braced him against the Henrietta feeding sign-up sheet. "You take that back! The Rangers are going all the way this year!"

"Oh, yeah?" Dweeb-a-saurus was getting brave. "You couldn't even win against a last-place team like Mount Carmel!"

"Hah!" I cried. "With our mascot, we're unbeatable!"

Zachary's eyes narrowed. An evil grin appeared on that smarmy face. "Well, how long do you think you're going to have her?" he taunted, pointing over at

Henrietta. "Look at her! She's almost full grown! As soon as she's an adult chicken, Milo's going to kill her and serve her up at the science fair!"

This came at a lull in the conversation, so Zachary's last words echoed through the lab as if they'd been broadcast over loudspeakers. A gasp went up like all the air was being sucked out of the room. I dropped the dweeb like a hot potato. All eyes turned from Zachary and me to Henrietta to Milo.

"Milo, is it true?" quavered Sheila Martel in disbelief.

"Of course not!" scoffed Kelly Marie. "How could it be true?"

But I took one look at Mrs. Baggio's stricken face and I knew something was wrong.

"Certainly it's true," Milo said. He seemed totally amazed that we even had to ask. "My project is on the food chain. The specimen is food. I've explained it several times."

"This isn't funny!" snapped Kelly Marie nervously. "Mrs. Baggio, make him cut it out!"

The Bag ordered everyone to their seats. "All right," she said, walking up and down in front of us. "This has gone far enough. We've all sort of adopted Henrietta as class pet. But let us never forget that she is Milo's project. The plan for her has always been the same: Throughout her life we have given her food. That food did not merely disappear. By the science of the food chain, it helped her grow from a chick to a hen. And it will resurface when the meat is eaten at the science fair."

The place went nuts. Everybody started babbling all at the same time. Kelly Marie was out of control, screaming at the top of her lungs. I guess I was pretty loud myself. Sheila was in tears, and Zachary was trying to offer support to Milo, who was shell-shocked. Even in the total chaos, Superdweeb couldn't resist the opportunity to suck up.

The Bag had climbed on top of the teacher's desk and was waving her arms in a desperate attempt to restore order. Fat chance. If St. Martin had been selected by the Air Force for target bombing, the class couldn't have been more upset.

Henrietta darted around her coop, knocking over get-well cards in agitation. You'd almost think she knew that she'd just been invited to lunch as the main course.

As for me, I was the most miserable guy in the place. How many times in the history of sports has a team lost a championship because somebody killed and ate their mascot?

It was Kelly Marie who finally shut us up, and she did it with a voice that would have put an air raid siren to shame:

"Quiet! QUI – ET!!!"

Silence fell. Even the Bag sat down. Kelly Marie faced

Milo in a gunfighter's stance. If looks could kill, California Boy would have made it to the cemetery in plenty of time to greet his chicken.

"Milo Neal," she began in a raspy voice that none of us even recognized. "The science fair is in less than three weeks. Are you telling me that Henrietta has two-and-a-half weeks to live?"

Milo looked pretty shaken as he spent too much time adjusting his Bertrand St. Rene glasses. "More or less," he admitted. "You have to allow time for Arno's Butcher Shop to prepare the meat."

"But class —" Mrs. Baggio made a feeble attempt to regain control.

"Don't worry, everybody!" Kelly Marie overpowered her. "It is *never* going to happen! Not in a million years!"

16

"PSYCHOLOGY TALK"
BY KELLY MARIE GINSBERG

Dear Mr. Delong,

As our principal, you're a pretty busy man, so
maybe you don't know that Milo Neal is planning a
brutal murder at your school...

I paused in front of my dad's typewriter. Was the
wording strong enough? I really needed to get his attention. I signed the letter and frowned. Maybe Mr. Delong
would think that stopping Milo would be meddling in
Mrs. Baggio's class. A lot of principals didn't like to do
that. With Henrietta's life hanging in the balance, I
couldn't risk it. I had to go to a higher authority.

Dear Mayor Troy,

    I'm writing for your help to stop a heinous crime
in St. Martin . . .

While sealing the envelope, I thought it over. The
mayor was one of those idiots who considered it great
PR for the town that Victor Neal's son was growing up
here. I remembered his picture in the paper right beside
Milo and his mom when they first moved back. Would
he have the guts to step in against Milo?

Dear Congressman Kovacs,

    I know it's a long flight from Washington and
kind of scary with blizzard season coming up. But
you are desperately needed here to save a life . . .

I pledged my entire Thanksgiving weekend to writing letters and making phone calls. Milo and his mom
went down to Minneapolis to stay with relatives, so
there was no point in picketing on their lawn. Mrs.
Baggio had Henrietta; I left sixteen messages on her an-
swering machine.

"Kelly!" my father called. "What happened to all the
stamps?"

"Just take it out of my allowance," I said readily.

The phone rang and I picked it up. It was Sheila from
science class. "Kelly Marie," she said, "would you be
willing to sign a petition to save Henrietta?"

"That's a great idea!" I exclaimed.

"It wasn't mine," she admitted. "I got it from Joey and Lynette."

"Joey and Lynette?" I repeated. "I thought they hated each other!"

"They were both so worried about Henrietta that they realized how short life can really be," Sheila explained. "They got back together and formed SMASH."

"SMASH?"

"Stop Milo And Save Henrietta. Aren't you a member?"

"Sign me up!" I cried. Deep inside, I doubted that a couple of airheads like Joey and Lynette could work up anything that might help Henrietta. But on the other hand, maybe two half-wits make up a whole. Anyway, the more people you had banging the drum, the better the chance of it reaching the right ear. Which gave me an idea:

Dear Governor Hutchinson,
   Some say that a society is judged by how it treats its weakest citizen. Well, what could be weaker than a chicken . . . ?

"Kelly," my mom called, "hurry up! We're going over to Grandma's!"

"I'm not going," I replied.

"What?" There were footsteps pounding up the stairs

and then my mom appeared in my doorway. "Aren't you feeling well?"

I looked at her earnestly. "Mom, what if at Grandma's I get this brilliant idea that would save Henrietta, but by the time I come home, I've forgotten it?"

She perched on the edge of my desk. "Now, Kelly, dear, we agree that the Neal boy's project goes too far. But that's up to Mrs. Baggio and the school, not to me and not to you. Besides, you're not a baby anymore. This happens. You remember when our spaniel died?"

"Mom, Oliver got run over by a station wagon. Nobody ate him!"

She sighed. "We can bring Dad's laptop computer to Grandma's. So if you have a breakthrough, you can jot it down."

She obviously didn't think I would take her up on it. But when Grandpa placed that cooked bird on the Thanksgiving table and started carving, I pushed my plate aside and powered up.

> Dear Minnesota Chapter ASPCA,
> Do you handle chickens? If so I have a tale to tell that will simply break your heart . . .

I attended the SMASH meeting at Lynette's house after the Rangers got home from their road trip on Saturday. The players were pretty up because they'd just scored a big win against a strong team from Rochester.

You didn't have to be a psychologist to figure out that Adam and those lunkheads cared a lot more about winning than they did about Henrietta, but I kept my mouth shut. I needed the Rangers on Henrietta's side.

"Milo wouldn't let us take Henrietta to an away game," Steve grumbled. "He's still mad about the party!"

"Look who's talking!" shrilled Lynette. "*He's* going to cook her for lunch and he's worried *we* won't take care of her!"

"So you guys won without Henrietta?" I asked in disbelief.

Steve shook his head. "She was there. But Milo had to come, too."

Adam grinned. "We stuck him on the bus beside DeeVee. Three hours of slap shot details."

"Serves him right," I grimaced. "I'd like to send *Milo* to the butcher shop!"

"I say he should be our target," Lafayette agreed. "Let's see him finish his science project with two broken arms!"

"Chill out," said Adam of all people. Since he was such a hockey nut, I figured he'd be screaming for Milo's blood louder than anybody else. "You can't hold it against Milo. He honestly thought we all knew what happens at the end of his project. And, face it — every time we started getting attached to the chicken, he warned us not to. He didn't even want us to name her."

"It's true," said Brendan mournfully. "He must have

said it a million times: 'A chicken is not a pet; a chicken is a chicken.' We didn't listen."

"Oh, shut up!" I snapped. "So he told us! That makes it right? Milo doesn't matter! The science fair doesn't matter! Your stupid hockey team doesn't matter! The only thing that matters is Henrietta!"

> Dear Mr. Arno,
>
> I happen to be a vegetarian and wouldn't eat meat if you paid me. But sometime in the middle of December, Milo Neal is going to bring you a chicken. I don't know how much money you butchers earn. But whatever Milo is paying you, I'll give you double not to kill it. Just bring the chicken to the above address. And whatever you do, don't tell Milo . . .

I lay awake Sunday night, tossing and turning. I wracked my brain. Had I done everything possible? Had I written everyone who had any power whatsoever to save Henrietta? Could there be a stone left unturned? An avenue unexplored? An authority I could still appeal to?

And then it came to me.

> Dear Victor Neal,
>
> I won't take up too much of your time because I know you must be pretty busy being a TV star and a scientific genius.

I am writing because I think you should know that your son has a big brain but a very small heart. And if he kills Henrietta, everybody in school is going to hate him. Please hurry. The science fair is on December 14th, but Henrietta could die any day now. You've got to do something!

Yours anxiously,
Kelly Marie Ginsberg

PS: Henrietta is a chicken.

17

EXPERIMENT NOTES: MILO NEAL
12/07

> I admit I was nervous about fitting in when I moved to St. Martin. But even in my wildest nightmares I never expected to be Public Enemy #1 by Christmas.

> Yet here I was, Milo the Merciless, heartless cold-blooded killer of poor defenseless small animals, chickens a specialty.

{How did I get into this mess? Was it my fault? Was it everybody else's?/further study req'd.}

> I kept analyzing the chain of events to try to detect the link where I went wrong. I mean, I did my proj. following the scientific method step by step. And now the whole school was up in arms over their "darling Henrietta." Logic says that someone must be crazy here. The question = Was it me?

{In Los Angeles the life of one little chicken wouldn't cause this much ruckus. But this ≠ Los Angeles. I noticed that when the temperature went down to eleven below zero last night!!!}

> Still, the Minnesota winter was balmy compared with the deep freeze I had to face every day at school. It had gone way beyond our little science class. The halls were plastered with SAVE HENRIETTA posters. Mr. Delong and the staff took them all down, but by 9:00 the next morning, they'd be up again. I saw one that featured my picture from the *Sentinel*, doctored up to make me look like a medieval executioner holding a giant beheading ax. Another said MILO with a red line through it, like a no smoking sign. Everywhere I looked, something about "chicken rights" was staring back at me. On Monday morning, we were all welcomed back from Thanksgiving weekend by a giant banner over the front entrance of the school: MAKE FRIENDS NOT CUTLETS.

> Didn't it figure? Even in a windchill of −40°, I couldn't get sick enough to miss a day of school.

> The only person who would walk with me, talk to me, and sit with me in the cafeteria was ZG. Just my luck. If there was anyone in all of St. Martin I'd have enjoyed being ignored by, it was him. He called it "friend loyalty," and although I had a bit of a problem with the "friend" part, he was definitely loyal.

"It's not your fault everybody else was too stupid to

understand your project," he told me several times that miserable week.

> Heaven help me — I was so shaken up that I appreciated having ZG to confide in.

"I don't know. Maybe it *is* my fault," I said. "Everybody else sees something special in that chicken."

"Not everybody," ZG offered. "I don't."

"Yes you do," I countered. "They see something to love; you see something to hate. I just see a link in the food chain. Why am I the only one?"

"Well," said ZG thoughtfully. "Have you tried?"

"Tried what?"

"Getting to know Henrietta."

"There's nothing to get to know!" I exploded.

> But that day after school, locked in my room, I made an effort. I sat cross-legged on the floor and stared into the cage. What I saw was really quite impressive. The creature that had been a tiny wisp of fluff a scant two months ago was now covered in lustrous white feathers. Her red comb was well-defined, and in spite of the setback, she was plump and healthy. She'd been on a full diet for two weeks now. In fact, my calculations had been remarkably accurate. The subj. was now a fully grown hen, ready for the dinner table —

> Wait a minute. The logical scientific approach was exactly what I was trying to avoid here. I needed to be

totally emotional about this if I was going to see what other people saw.

> I said, "Okay, Henrietta —" Yes, I broke my own rule and called the spec. Henrietta, "Okay . . . uh . . . sweetie, strut your stuff."

> She clucked, she twitched, and she bobbed her head up and down like chickens do. There was no recognition of me as the caregiver. None of the personality KMG seemed to see, no sign of the keen intelligence so obvious to JS, not a trace of the fun-loving *joie de vivre* that won LM's heart. I didn't feel inspired like the hockey team. I didn't even observe anything to dislike, à la ZG. She was, all things considered, a chicken — subj., spec., link in the food chain, the wind beneath nobody's wings.

> CONCLUSION: I'm not the one out of step with the band; they're all out of step with me.

> There was a knock on my bedroom door. I leaped to my feet as my mother let herself in. "Milo, may I have a word with you?"

{A word usually meant five hundred thousand million words +/− 10%/further study req'd.}

"Sure, Mom. What's up?"

"I just got off the phone with Mr. Delong," she said worriedly. "He told me what's been going on at school. And he suggested I talk to you about changing the experiment."

I stuck out my jaw. "How?"

"By eliminating the part where you eat Henrietta."

"That *is* the experiment, Mom!" I exclaimed. "There *is* nothing else! I can't change it!"

"You mean you won't."

I tried to be patient. "If you order a cheeseburger, hold the bun, hold the cheese, hold the meat, you've got a handful of nothing, right? Well, that's what you're left with when you have a food chain experiment that defies the food chain!"

My mother sighed. "Mr. Delong said the whole school is up in arms over your project. Some of the kids are so upset that their parents are calling the office to complain. They've even had a call from the *Sentinel*. Milo, I grew up in St. Martin. It's not like Los Angeles, where something like this would barely be noticed. These are nice, warm people — but if this story gets around, you may never live it down! Please, just this once I want you to give in."

I folded my arms in front of me. "And take an incomplete in science?"

"Mr. Delong said you'd get an A. And they'd still pick you for the science fair."

"It would be an incomplete to *me!*" I insisted. "They could give me Dad's Nobel Prize and it would still be for an unfinished project!"

She looked at me very seriously. "I admire your integrity, but I think you're making a big mistake over something that's just not that important." And she let herself quietly out of my room.

> Mom has a nasty habit of cutting the legs out from under you just when you think you're on solid ground.

> I looked to the cage and this time I really wanted it. I truly, honestly was dying to see even the slightest indication that there was somebody in there. The specimen twitched and warbled. Nobody home.

> Deep down, I knew Mom was right. I was as cooked as the subj. was going to be. Except — here in St. Martin, all I had of my dad was the stuff he taught me about experiments and scientific method. I was out of his life completely. But if I could win the science fair, that = one huge reminder that I was his son. I would almost be following in his footsteps! Maybe then he'd call more often and come to see me — even invite me back to California for a long visit.

> This was more than a science fair to me. It = a chance to start over with my father.

> Even with all the tension at home and at school, nothing compared to the pure, unadulterated agony of the hockey games. I couldn't very well relinquish my subj. to those well-meaning lunatics. Which meant that I had to accompany the spec. to the rink. I suppose I could have refused. But I was so hated already, I didn't dare make things worse. There I'd sit, LM despising me

on the left, KMG reviling me from the right, watching a sport that made as much sense to me as a pet rock.

So I didn't complain too much when AL told me that Saturday's game would be in Fairmont, about thirty miles away. And when I found out that this match would determine the South Minnesota championship, I allowed myself a faint glimmer of hope. Please, oh please let the team win! Then they'd be happy, they'd no longer need my chicken, and maybe, just maybe that might ease some of the pressure at school.

> The bus ride was pure torture — thirty minutes in a confined space with large people who hated me. It was far worse than the games themselves, where the players' dirty looks were covered by their visors. At one point I heard LH trying to convince DeeVee to take a slap shot at my head.

> I didn't think it was very funny, but it drew a big guffaw from Coach C. "Are you kidding? If Vincent could *aim* that thing, he'd be in the NHL!"

"I don't have to be here at all—" I announced to the bus.

"Who sent for you?" came a chorus of snarls from above the shoulder pads.

"— and neither does this cage," I finished.

Coach C broke the unpleasant standoff. "All right, listen up," he ordered. "You all know where we stand. Fairmont's in first place with a record of fourteen and five. We're half a game behind them at thirteen and five with one tie. Which means a tie still leaves us in second place. We have to go for the win."

"We're gonna crush those guys!" roared LH, and the entire team joined in a bloodcurdling roar. The coach beamed with pride.

> Why did athletes feel the need to rampage like gorillas in order to prepare for a game?/further study req'd. I had a vision of the Fairmont Flyers in *their* locker room, beating their breasts and howling in honor of our arrival.

> Their fans were certainly in a state of high excitement. I was appalled by the hostile reaction the Rangers received when they took the ice.

But when I mentioned it to Coach C, he looked at me as if I'd just arrived from Mars. "They're *supposed* to hate us, Neal! We're the other team!"

"Ah," I replied. "Much like the resentment of rival scientists when my father won his Nobel Prize."

> His response was a look blank enough to use as a billboard.

> Before the opening face-off, I had to hold my spec. over the bench so the players could bonk their helmets into the cage and run their sticks along the bars.

"Go get 'em, Henrietta," breathed AL, his face so intense it was almost scary.

"It's all up to you, girl," added JS.

{Was I missing something? How was it possible for my subj. to influence the outcome of a sporting event?

Especially when she was in a cage, outside the field of play/further study req'd.}

> Of course, I was not the best person to judge a game of ice hockey. What I saw best resembled a riot on ice. Upon closer inspection, I discovered the puck, which told the combatants whom to brutalize. When somebody scored, his entire team would perform the Minnesota equivalent of an earthquake. I got the impression that these two schools were evenly matched, since the earthquakes took place equally often on each bench.

> How was it that I could understand high-level science but couldn't make heads or tails of the chaos on the ice?/further study req'd. I concentrated on the scoreboard. At least that way I would know who was winning. Although it looked like nobody was going to win this game. When the clock ticked down to the final minute, the score was deadlocked 7–7.

> I suppose it was the thought that the season was nearly over that induced me to try to make up with the hockey team. "Congratulations on a well-played game," I called down to the bench. "You can be really proud of a tie against such a strong opponent."

The coach stared at me. "Neal, are you out of your mind?"

"Milo, you big dope!" AL shouted up at me. "A tie does us *nothing!* We need a win or Fairmont takes the championship!"

Coach C shifted into high gear. "Lurie, Sorrentino, get

in there! Pull the goalie! Put Hughes in the slot! Tell Tenorio to pinch!"

> No, I don't have a clue what any of that meant. When the puck was dropped, all that strategy boiled down to this: Both teams stampeded the Fairmont net. They met with a resounding crunch that shook the building. There they lay, piled up like sandbags, three feet in front of the empty Flyers goal.

> There was an enormous gasp from the crowd. Maybe they were searching for the puck, which had disappeared under the mountain of fallen players. Silence followed as the Rangers looked on in desperation, their championship hopes down to the final dwindling seconds on the clock.

> And suddenly there it was! At the edge of the pile, just beyond AL's shoulder — the puck!

"Adam, behind you!" I shouted.

> Lying flat on his stomach under two Fairmont players, AL pulled his stick around, sliding it blindly along the ice. It batted into the puck with a tiny clink. Slowly — agonizingly slowly — the puck trickled over the goal line into the net.

The buzzer sounded to end the game. Final score: 8–7 for the South Minnesota champion Rangers.

"But Adam!" I insisted for the twentieth time on the bus ride home. "It was me! _I_ was the one who yelled, 'Behind you!'"

> I don't know why I cared so much. Maybe I felt that if I was going to get involved in anything as meaning-less as an ice hockey game, I should at least get some credit for it.

"Milo, give it a rest," AL groaned, absently stroking my spec.'s feathers. For some reason, they had switched places between their trophy and my chicken. The cham-pionship cup was locked in the cage. "You weren't even watching the game!"

"At the end I was!" I defended myself. "How else could I have seen the puck in the scramble?"

"Your voice is too high," JS insisted. "The guy who yelled was, you know, *deeper.*"

"A baritone," agreed Brendan.

"No, it was *higher,*" ST argued. "Higher, and kind of raspy, like an old guy."

"It was *me!*" I cried. {These hockey players could be maddeningly stubborn/further study req'd.}

AL handed my spec. over the seat and regarded me with genuine pity in his eyes. "You don't have to *lie,* Milo."

"If you're trying to make us love you, forget it," snarled LH. "Nobody will ever forgive you for what you're going to do to Henrietta!"

I sighed in defeat. "Well, at least she's not your mas-cot anymore. That ought to make it a little easier."

JS stared at me. "Are you nuts?"

I spread my arms wide. "The season just ended!"

AL faced me. "Milo, we're South Minnesota champions! We have to play the Canadians next Saturday! We can't face them without Henrietta!"

"But — but —" I stammered. I couldn't remember being at such a loss for words since the day my parents told me they were splitting up. "But the science fair is next Saturday. The specimen won't — I mean, she can't —" A chorus of outrage cut me off.

> Next year my science proj. isn't going to involve any type of life-form unless it's already dead before it can develop a fan club. The total irony was that, if I had kept my eyes on the scoreboard instead of the ice, I never would have spotted that loose puck. Ergo, I couldn't have shouted to AL, and the clock *and* the season would have expired with the score still tied 7–7. No championship, no Canadians, no date with destiny for my chicken.

> It was undeniable. Victor Neal's son, the genius-in-training, had grown up to be the biggest idiot on the face of the earth.

> Maybe I was adopted/further study req'd.

18 🐔

DOWNLOADED FROM THE FILES
OF ZACHARY GUSTAFSON

HORRORDOME

[SCENE 4]

[INTERIOR: Goodyear blimp – day]

High above the Enormo-Dome, the brilliant but warped evil scientist DR. DEMENTO finishes tying up the BLIMP PILOT.

PILOT

You'll never get away with this! You're demented!

DR. DEMENTO

No, I'm Dement-*o!*

He stuffs a gag in the PILOT's mouth and throws his
head back in terrifying maniacal laughter.

[POINT-OF-VIEW SHOT: Far below, thousands of people, like ants, stream into the 100,000-seat stadium.]

DR. DEMENTO

Poor unsuspecting fools! I'll fill their "Super Bowl" with
the hot soup of terror!

As the last few stragglers enter the stadium, he presses
a red button.

The giant retractable roof of the stadium slams shut
and all entrances seal automatically. A hundred thousand people are trapped!

I rubbed my hands together with glee. This stuff
practically wrote itself! This was going to be my best
screenplay ever! Dr. Demento was a truly memorable
character. I could easily see a whole series of movies:
Horrordome II: The Carnage Continues; *Horrordome
III: The Meadowlands Massacre*; the possibilities were
endless.

Perfect timing, too. Pretty soon I'd be close enough
to Milo to ask his dad to show my work around in
Hollywood. Spilling the beans about Henrietta croaking
was one of my smarter moves. I can't believe I didn't
think of it sooner! How do you get to be somebody's
best friend? By making everyone else in the world hate

him! It was friendship by default. Milo was alone like a dog except for me.

I know that sounds cold. But I was a good friend to Milo. For instance, I told him about the time I wet my pants at Disney World, because friends always share their deepest secrets. He's probably going to tell me something important, too. I went over to his house every day that week. I mean, the guy needed the support. Even his own mother wanted to stop him from whacking Henrietta. I give him credit, though. He was brave. Every single day he tried to talk me out of coming, saying it wasn't necessary and stuff.

"Oh, it's no problem," I told him. "I'm here for you, buddy." He just groaned with gratitude.

School was the toughest of all. It wasn't easy sharing a classroom with a doomed chicken. The air in the lab crackled with tension and heartbreak and anger. Every few minutes, someone would look over at Henrietta poking around in her coop and freak out, or burst into tears, or launch into yet another plea for mercy.

They all knew Henrietta was close to the end, because the science fair was on Saturday. But Mrs. Baggio banned all Henrietta talk, and Milo wouldn't say when he was taking that lousy chicken over to Arno's Butcher Shop. So nobody knew when "it" was going to happen.

I did, of course. I read it right off Mrs. Neal's kitchen calendar last night. There it was, in bright red ink under Wednesday — *Arno's 4 P.M.*

Milo caught me snooping and swore me to secrecy.

"Hey, you can trust me, pal," I pledged.

Zachary Gustafson's word is as good as gold. I only slipped up once, but I think I got away with it.

I committed the strategic error of being in the washroom at the same time as Adam on Tuesday before science. As usual, he started getting on my case about taking Milo's side against his stupid Rangers. I wasn't in the mood for another wedgie, so I told him to mind his own business.

"It *is* my business!" he snapped back. "It's the captain's business to make sure our mascot is safe!"

So help me, I couldn't resist. "After tomorrow," I assured him, "you won't have to worry anymore."

I left him standing there in the can. I was positive he didn't understand what I meant. These hockey players aren't too bright, you know.

Just to be sure, I kept an eye on him in class. He was looking back at Henrietta a lot. Did he suspect anything? Probably not. Everybody was looking at Henrietta — everybody except Milo.

Mrs. Baggio was still trying to run this like a normal class. The science projects were starting to come in, but it was taking forever to present them. Sheila sobbed her way through her project on bats, never once taking her eyes off the chicken coop in the corner.

"Bravo!" Kelly Marie leaped to her feet, applauding madly. "That's the greatest science project I've ever seen

in my life! Mrs. Baggio, 'Bats' should be our class entry for the science fair."

"It's awesome!" Adam chimed in. "I never knew science could be so exciting!"

By then the whole class was clued in. They were clapping and chanting, "Bats! Bats! Bats! . . ."

I sprang up. "This is stupid! They don't think 'Bats' is any good. They just want someone else to go to the science fair instead of Milo so there's no sense cooking Henrietta!" I sat down amidst a shower of spitballs and jeers.

Mrs. Baggio put on a brave face. "The student who goes to the science fair will be the one who hands in the best work. And that decision won't be made until all the projects are in."

She was in for a long wait because I hadn't started mine yet. It wasn't that I was lazy; I just didn't have the guts to ask Mrs. Baggio to remind me what my topic was. But I wasn't worried. I'd whip something up at three o'clock in the morning on the last day. How hard could it be for the best friend of Victor Neal's son?

[INTERIOR: Enormo-Dome – day]

Halftime at the Super Bowl. The MARCHING BAND is on the field. MAJORETTES are twirling batons. The CROWD is clapping along.

[INTERIOR: Goodyear blimp – day]

DR. DEMENTO prepares for the final phase of his sinister experiment.

DR. DEMENTO

They called me mad when I proposed the transmutation of matter! But I'll show them all! They'll see that Myron Demento is nobody's fool!

> He flips a giant switch.

> [INTERIOR: Enormo-Dome – day]

> There is a brilliant flash and a thunderclap. The cheering sound has changed to a high-pitched warble. The music stops; the instruments fall to the Astroturf.

> The smoke clears to reveal the stadium, filled with 100,000 chickens. Chickens fill the stands. The BAND and MAJORETTES have changed into chickens. Chickens wait in line at the concession stands. In the broadcast booth, chicken COMMENTATORS cluck into the microphones. The TEAMS try to take the field but, now chickens, they can barely move inside their helmets. Chicken REFEREES flop about, lost in giant striped shirts . . .

Whoa!

It was happening again! More chickens! A hundred thousand of them this time!

In a cold sweat, I switched off the computer. Was I losing my mind? Just when I needed to be in peak writing form, my whole style was going to the dogs! Or, at the very least, the chickens! How could I give Victor Neal a screenplay full of chickens?

Okay, calm down, I told myself. It was only the big ruckus at school giving me chickens on the brain. Tomorrow Milo would take Henrietta to Arno's and it was a one-way trip. She'd be gone — from my life *and* my writing. Aloha, my feathered friend.

What a beautiful thought! Only — it had seemed a lot more beautiful when it wasn't happening *tomorrow*.

I struggled into my pajamas, figuring I'd go to bed really early and sleep off this weird feeling. But when I was all tucked in and the lights were out, it wasn't any better. I kept seeing Henrietta — and an ax — and a rotating spit. I should have been overjoyed about this. I hated the chicken and the chicken hated me. This was the perfect ending to a horrible relationship, especially since I wasn't the one who was going to die.

Get a grip, Zachary!

Every time I closed my eyes I saw that silly red craw that wiggled when she walked on those stupid chicken feet; that annoying squawk echoed in my head; those beady eyes stared at me — reproachfully —

And I knew, as sure as Hollywood is in California, that if I let Henrietta die, she was going to haunt me for the rest of my life.

I jumped out of bed and started throwing on clothes.

Fade to black . . .

19

RANGERS UPDATE:
CAPTAIN ADAM LURIE REPORTING

After tomorrow you won't have to worry anymore.

That was what the dweeb said. But what did it mean? Was Milo planning to back off and let the chicken live? That didn't sound like Milo. And it definitely didn't sound like a twenty-time recipient of the Congressional Medal of Losers. No, Zachary meant I wouldn't have to worry because there would be no more chicken to worry about. Tomorrow was execution day!

Well, I didn't know if Henrietta was special or just some Joe Blow chicken off any farm. But I was sure of one thing: I had to save the team. And saving the team meant saving the bird.

So that's what I was doing when I headed for the school at eight o'clock Tuesday night. Chicken napping.

I knew the janitor's entrance would be unlocked until the custodian left around nine. The tricky part was avoiding Mr. Farr as I crept through the maze of tall storage shelves and slipped into the main hallway of the school. Mr. Farr was a nice guy, but I didn't want to have to explain what I was doing there. This was exactly the kind of caper that could get you kicked off the team.

It went so smoothly that I let down my guard and I almost missed it. For there, in the gleaming wetness of the freshly mopped floor, was a trail of sneaker footprints. I frowned. It definitely wasn't Mr. Farr — the prints were too small. It didn't make sense. There weren't any clubs or teams that met on Tuesday nights. Who, besides me, was sneaking around the school?

Keeping a sharp eye out for Mr. Farr, I followed the trail. It stretched past the gym, through the math wing — I froze. The intruder, whoever it was, was heading for the science lab.

Panicking, I picked up speed and made for the Bag's room on the dead run. As I raced around the last corner, I never saw the foot that tripped me.

To say I flew forty feet would be exaggerating, but not by much.

WUMP!

I hit the ground and saw stars. When my vision cleared, the person standing over me was Kelly Marie.

She was smiling. "Adam," she said proudly, "you came to save Henrietta."

I sat up and faced her. "That's what I *was* doing be-fore some *total maniac* tried to kill me!"

She hauled me up. "Well, I couldn't tell it was you until you were flat on your face already." It was perfect commando logic.

"How did you know tonight was the last chance?" I asked. "Did the dweeb spill his guts to you, too?"

"I got my mom to call Arno's and say she was Mrs. Neal," Kelly Marie admitted. "They confirmed the ap-pointment for four o'clock tomorrow."

"Right after school!" I gulped. The Rangers were that close to losing our mascot! "Come on, let's go get her."

We ran into the lab together and stood, side by side, staring in shock. The coop was empty.

I was pretty upset, but Kelly Marie went into a meltdown. Her face turned bright red and she began to hyperventilate, each breath making a high-pitched wheezing whistle.

"Not so loud!" I hissed. "Do you want Mr. Farr on our necks?"

"But where's Henrietta?"

"I don't know! How should I know?" I babbled, straining to keep my voice down. "Unless Milo antici-pated our move and took her home a day early."

It took a second to recognize her reaction, because it wasn't rage, or a tantrum, or a psychology lecture. Her lips trembled and tears rolled down her cheeks. Kelly Marie was *crying!*

I hate crying. "Cut that out," I ordered nervously.

"She's *go-o-o-one!*" she quavered.

Tears freak me out. For a moment, I even forgot about the Rangers and how much we needed Henrietta. I was *so* uncomfortable I didn't know where to look — up at the ceiling, out the window, down at the floor — I gawked.

"You're wearing your Doc Martens!"

She belted me right in the face. "How can you talk about shoes when we've lost Henrietta, you cold-hearted —"

"No, no, no!" I grabbed her by the shoulders. "The footprints I followed were sneaker prints! So they can't be yours! They had to be —"

"Milo's!" she finished breathlessly.

We both looked down. The tracks led from the doorway to the chicken wire, then away from the coop straight into Mrs. Baggio's equipment closet.

I was over there in two strides. "Okay, Milo, the jig's up. Come on out."

There was no answer, so Kelly Marie rushed up and flung open the door. But it wasn't Milo in there, clutching the struggling Henrietta to his chest. Among the beakers and experiment books cowered none other than His Royal Loserness, the gold medalist from the Loser Olympics, Zachary Gustafson.

"Are you taking her to Milo?" I accused.

"I'm rescuing her!" the dweeb insisted.

"Don't believe him," snarled Kelly Marie. "He hates Henrietta."

"Darn right," he said proudly. "But do you think I want to spend the rest of my life with *that* face on my conscience?" To prove his innocence, he handed the bird to Kelly Marie.

As a parting shot, Henrietta took a swipe at him with her claw.

"Ow!"

I clamped my hand over the dweeb's mouth. "Pipe down and let's get out of here!" I grabbed a blanket and wrapped it around our mascot.

Once outside the school, we paused to consider Henrietta's future.

"I'll take her," Kelly Marie said immediately.

"You're the first person Milo will suspect," I told her. "And I'm the second." I turned to face Zachary.

"No way!" cried Kelly Marie. "I refuse to leave Henrietta with someone who hates her!"

"She hated me first!" whined Zachary.

"It's perfect," I argued. "Everybody knows Zack and Henrietta hate each other. Plus he's such a big suck-up that no one would believe he'd ever go against Milo."

"That's not fair!" said Zachary hotly. "Milo and I have a genuine friendship!"

Kelly Marie addressed the bird. "It's okay, sweetie.

He may be a complete idiot, but he isn't going to let anybody hurt you." She shook her fist at the dweeb. "Right, Zachary?"

I glanced at my watch. It was almost nine. "Let's get home before our parents start thinking something's up."

I looked into Superloser's shifty eyes. "The Canadians game is on Saturday afternoon. If anything happens to the bird between now and then, *you're* going to take her place at Arno's Butcher Shop."

20 🐔

DOWNLOADED FROM THE FILES
OF ZACHARY GUSTAFSON

How would Steven Spielberg smuggle a chicken into the house with his mom right there in the kitchen? I tried to use my screenwriter's imagination. In a real Hollywood movie, I would parachute into the reservoir in frogman gear, swim until the pipes got too skinny, and then rocket straight in through my bedroom window using antigravity boots. But in cheapo St. Martin, I didn't have any of that stuff. So I went to the garage, stuffed Henrietta into a cardboard carton, and got psyched up to finesse my way into the house.

Mom was doing the dishes — with her back to the hall — so I made a mad dash for the stairs.

"Zachary —"

Caught!

"I was on the phone with Laura Walters tonight, and she mentioned Brendan is working on a science project. Aren't you in that class?" Then Mom turned around and noticed the box. "Oh — what have you got there?"

"It's . . . it's . . . my science project."

She beamed. "That's great, hon. What's the topic?"

At that moment, Henrietta started scrambling around. Thinking fast, I pretended to lose control of the box to cover the movement. But no one could think fast enough to explain the long feather that came flying out and drifted to the floor.

Mom stared. "Your project is on feathers?"

"Oh . . . of course not . . . ha, ha. That wouldn't be very scientific. It's on —" I wracked my brain "— pens."

She goggled. "Pens?"

"You know," I explained, "like the first pens used to be feathers? A history of pens."

"That's wonderful!" she approved. "In fact, I think Dad has a fountain pen that would be perfect for your display."

I manufactured a yawn. "Maybe I should call it a night, Mom. I'm pretty tired."

I was almost home free, halfway up the stairs, when that miserable chicken squawked.

Mom was on me again. "Did you say something, dear?"

"Just yawning, Mom. Man, I'm beat."

"Be sure to hold the box steady," she cautioned. "I think some of your pens are rolling around."

I sprinted up the stairs and stuffed Henrietta's box under the bed. I felt like I'd just been dragged forty miles by horses. But deep down I knew the hassles were only beginning.

Mrs. Baggio made an impassioned speech first thing Wednesday morning. "I know that some of you may think it was kind to steal Henrietta and hide her away. But please remember that a lot of work went into Milo's project, whatever your opinion of it. It isn't fair to have it snatched away at the last minute."

The interrogation continued with Mr. Delong. "Boys and girls, it's important that you realize this is a *crime*. Henrietta is *property*. If she's not returned, we'll have no choice but to call in the police."

Then Milo made a little speech, but he was pretty low-key. He just kind of apologized for upsetting everybody with his project. "When I moved to St. Martin, I didn't want to make people hate me. Considering who my dad is, you know that science is really important to me. So I hope that whoever has my specimen will let me complete the experiment."

You could tell he was pretty fried. His expression was really downcast, and he headed home just before lunch, mumbling something about stomach cramps. I felt like worm guts, and Milo didn't even have to give me that look down his nose.

Kelly Marie shared none of my guilt. "Give me a break! Even now he's talking about 'the experiment' and 'the specimen.' To say he's a cold-hearted pig is an insult to pigs!"

"Don't blow it," Adam advised me. "The team knows you've got Henrietta, but everybody else is in the dark. So just play dumb. It should be easy for you."

You had to love that heartfelt gratitude.

In the halls at class changes, the name Henrietta was on everyone's lips. The relief was so thick that you could almost spread it on toast. There was a lot of speculation about the identity of the hero who saved Henrietta from the ax.

"It must be Kelly Marie. She's ballistic over that chicken!"

"It's got to be one of the Rangers! They stink without their mascot!"

"Mr. Delong snatched her to keep the peace at school."

"I'll bet Milo did it himself so he wouldn't have to kill her."

"No way! Lynette made Joey do it! The chicken's hidden in her attic!"

Notice that the name "Zachary Gustafson" never got mentioned by anybody. Like I wasn't cool enough to kidnap a chicken! I hate this school!

Dewey seemed to think that Henrietta was some new kind of fellow baby. He loved to sit under my bed and peek at her through the airholes in the box. When I took her out, he'd try to flap his arms and squawk along with her. She liked him, too. Or at least she didn't try to peck his head off like she did to me.

I figured there wasn't any harm in it. I mean, the kid couldn't talk and tell Mom. And anyway, when Dooms-day was mugging at that stupid bird, it kept him from bombing my computer. It was a whole new side of my baby brother. I'd always known he was homicidal, but now I saw he was stupid, too.

My dad came to the same conclusion at dinner on Thursday night. "What's wrong with the baby? He sounds like a chicken!"

My mother laughed. "He's just finding his voice."

"And the thing with the arms?"

I stepped in. "He's a baby, Dad. Babies do stuff like that."

Mom glowed with pride. She thought Doomsday and I were developing brotherly love. If she knew why —

My dad reached into his shirt pocket. "Here you go, Zachary. I brought a couple more pens for your project. Check out the green felt-tip. My boss's husband donated it to the cause."

"How's that project coming, anyway?" Mom asked. "You seem to be spending a lot of time locked in your room working on it."

"Oh, yeah!" I enthused. "It should be ready to hand in tomorrow." *Please don't ask to see it!*

The doorbell rang. My life was saved.

It was Kelly Marie. This was the fourth time in two days that she'd shown up on my doorstep. My folks were positive I had a girlfriend.

I took her up to my room to commune with "sweetie."

"Mr. Delong called the cops on me," she said, absently tapping Henrietta's beak with her Greenpeace pinky ring. "They sent this deputy over to my house to tell my parents I might be guilty of cattle rustling."

"Cattle rustling?" I repeated. "She's a chicken, not a cow!"

"It's just a bunch of legal mumbo jumbo," she shrugged. "Any theft of animals comes under this 1870 law that was written during the Old West days. Ignore it."

"That's easy for you to say," I pointed out. "You're not the one with the rustled cattle living under your bed!"

But she just played with Henrietta. The doorbell rang, and a moment later, another cattle rustler, Adam, joined us upstairs.

"Your folks went out to get some groceries. They took the little dweeb." He looked down at the chicken cradled in Kelly Marie's arms. "Hi, Henrietta. Ready for the Canadians?"

Kelly Marie bristled. "She's not going to that game! It isn't safe!"

"Hey!" Adam stuck out his jaw. "You might have saved this tweety-bird because you love her; *I* saved her for the Rangers."

"But she'll be caught!" Kelly Marie wrapped her arms protectively around Henrietta. "Someone'll see her on the bench and tell Milo!"

"We'll hide her in the spare equipment bag where we keep the extra pads," Adam explained. "No one'll see her."

"It's too risky!"

Adam folded his arms. "Either she goes to the big game or to Milo's." He added, "Tonight."

"You wouldn't!"

The doorbell interrupted the confrontation. I ran to the window and looked down at the porch. "It's Milo!"

"We've got to get out of here!" Adam exclaimed in a panic.

"Why?" asked Kelly Marie. "So we're visiting Zachary. Big deal."

"Get real! I'm on the *team*! I don't hang out with just anybody! A smart guy like Milo would see something was up!"

I started out of the room. "You two sit tight and shut up. And that goes double for the chicken. I'll see what he wants."

I opened the door and let Milo in. He looked awful.

"Sorry to bother you, Zachary," he said sadly. "I just had to get out of the house. Not even my mom is on my side these days."

I hesitated. For months I'd been waiting for Milo to turn to me as a true friend. Now, finally, it was happening. But I had two cattle rustlers and a hot chicken stashed in my room, and all I could think of was how to get rid of him.

But Milo was already shrugging off his jacket. "Mrs. Baggio phoned me today. She asked me to go to the science fair anyway. She said I should serve Real Dixie Fried Chicken as a symbol of my specimen's place in the food chain."

We sat down in the kitchen.

"I thought she wasn't deciding who goes to the science fair until all the projects were finished," I commented.

"Well, they're all in except one," he replied. "I saw the sheet. Someone's doing infrared astronomy."

"Oh, no!" It hit me like a blow to the head. *That* was my topic! "Are you sure it didn't say, you know — 'Pens'?"

He blinked. "Pens? You mean ancient methods of written communication like hieroglyphics and cuneiform?"

"No, I mean pens — like Bic," I sighed. "And Papermate."

155

"Oh. Well, no, it was definitely infrared astronomy. Anyway, I've decided to go with the fried chicken thing."

"It sounds great," I managed, not really paying attention. I was wracking my brain to come up with a way to convince Mrs. Baggio that infrared astronomy really meant pens.

"I haven't got a prayer without my specimen," Milo groaned. "It's just that, if I won here and did well at state, I might have qualified for the national." His eyes took on a faraway look. "That's in L.A. this year. I could have visited my dad."

"That would be . . . uh . . . really . . . uh . . . great . . . uh . . ." I didn't even know what I was saying. Because over Milo's left shoulder I could see Adam and Kelly Marie tiptoeing down the stairs and sneaking out the side door.

Milo kept talking.

Fade to black . . .

21

EXPERIMENT NOTES: MILO NEAL
12/14

> Riddle: How many Minnesotans does it take to kidnap a chicken?

Answer: Just one. But . . . *who?*

> Okay, it wasn't very funny. But it got me through the three toughest days of my life. Days where every face in the school hall seemed like it could belong to a potential spec.-napper. Days where I couldn't walk past a simple innocent house in St. Martin without wondering if my subj. was being held within.

> The interesting part was that I didn't really care anymore. I no longer lay awake at night wondering if the culprit = KMG, AL, or Sheila M; JS and/or LM; a hockey player, or some die-hard chicken activist I didn't even know. I forgave them all individually and blamed the

town. St. Martin, Minnesota, killed my proj. It was the fault of this small frostbitten city that I was about to pass off a bucket of Real Dixie Fried Chicken {extra crispy} as a science experiment.

"It's better this way," my mother assured me.

> Better for who?/further study req'd.

> But my sarcastic reply was interrupted by the phone. Probably ZG, to see when I was going over to the Community Center. He had volunteered to hang out with me at the science fair — big surprise. Actually, I was happy to have company. I didn't want to face the judges alone with my non-proj.

"Milo —" my mom called from the kitchen phone.

"It's almost time to go," I reminded her.

"It's your father."

> Sonic the Hedgehog wouldn't have beaten me to the receiver. My dad was usually so busy that these calls could be kind of rare.

"Hi, son. Freezing yet?" {This = his standard greeting ever since we moved to Minnesota.}

"Only since Labor Day," I grinned. The phone connection was fuzzy and distorted. "Where are you?"

"Twenty-seven thousand feet over Iowa," came the reply. "I'm on the plane, Milo. I should make it to the science fair in time for the judging."

> *Yes!!* My heart raced. I hadn't seen my father since September, except on TV. Only — suddenly, I remembered my proj. Victor Neal wasn't going to be very im-

pressed by a few notes and a bucket of fast food. "Uh, Dad, I just want to warn you —"

A burst of static came over the line. "I'm losing you, son. What did you say?"

"Just that my project got kind of messed up," I said, raising my voice. {Why does it always feel as if shouting will improve a bad connection? It has no scientific basis /further study req'd.} "It's kind of a long story —"

But I don't think my father could hear me. He said, "Blasted phone!" and the line went dead.

"He's coming?" my mother asked.

> When I nodded she smiled. A *real* smile. I appreciated that.

> For four months I'd been dying for my dad to visit. And now he was finally coming — just in time to see me disgrace the Neal family name in the field of science, which = his life's work.

> For some crazy reason, I couldn't wait to tell ZG. Out of all the people I knew in Minnesota *and* California, he'd be the only one to see the irony.

22 🐔

RANGERS UPDATE:
CAPTAIN ADAM LURIE REPORTING

The first scary thing about playing the Canadians was watching them arrive. Have you ever seen twenty gorillas get off a bus? It gives you a sick feeling in the pit of your stomach. And when you see the occasional little guy in there, you're thinking how fast or how good he must be, or what an amazing shot he must have to make the best junior high team in Winnipeg.

If you think I was nervous, you should have seen Brendan. I was afraid he'd melt onto the blacktop of the Community Center parking lot.

"Are you sure these guys are our age?" he babbled, his face green. "Maybe they sent a high school team by mistake! Look, that one has a mustache!"

"It's just a little dirt on his face," I said quietly.

"See? They don't wash! They're like cave people! That

one looks like Arnold Schwarzenegger! I can't play these guys! They'll score fifty on me!"

"Don't talk like that!" snapped Steve. "We won the championship with you!"

"You won the championship *in spite of* me!" Brendan corrected bitterly.

"You're the Wall," I insisted. But deep down I knew he'd never be the real Wall — never measure up to his brother. He was trying; he was a great kid. But that didn't stop pucks. Watching the Canadians lumbering into the Community Center, I realized those giants were going to eat Brendan for lunch.

Laffy cleared his throat carefully. "I talked to Coach Crenshaw after school yesterday. He said these guys are the Red River Junior High Rebels. Remember St. Boniface who skunked us last year? Well, the Rebels beat them by five goals."

"Thanks," said Joey sarcastically. He looked terrible. Tension over Henrietta and the big game had brought about another breakup with Lynette.

"Look," I said, "none of this stuff should be a great shock. We knew the Canadians were going to be awesome. What did you expect? A bunch of shrimps in ballet tutus?"

"No," Brendan replied, "but —"

"Let's all calm down," I interrupted. "Go home for lunch. I'll see you guys back here at game time."

My confidence was all fake. Lunch may as well have been fried Styrofoam for all I tasted it. I couldn't relax. And I was practically a wreck by the time I arrived at La Casa Loser to pick up Henrietta for the game.

I found Zachary the same way. "My mom's on the warpath," he admitted, his face turned away from Henrietta's flapping wings as he pulled her box out from under his bed. "She found out I got a D-minus-minus on 'A History of Pens.'"

I unzipped the spare equipment bag, which was Henrietta's golden carriage to the ball. "What did you expect? It was garbage."

"*I'm* pretty happy with it," the dweeb told me. "I expected to get an F."

I picked up Henrietta. She seemed to be in a peculiar mood today, flapping her wings and resisting my grip. "What's with the bird?" I grimaced, stuffing her in the duffle.

He shrugged. "She's like that every day for me."

Crash! All of a sudden, a little Hot Wheels car came flying out of nowhere and bounced off the computer on Zachary's desk. My eyes shifted to the doorway. There stood Dewey Gustafson — the microdweeb — his arm cocked back to throw another car.

"*Doomsday!!*" Zachary hurled himself in front of the computer. While in midair, he reached out an arm and knocked down the flying toy.

"Go, Zack," I laughed. Whoever would have expected such a big loser to pull off a slick athletic move? Seriously, that was highlight-film stuff!

But the baby wasn't done yet. He had a whole pile of cars at his feet, and he threw them all at the computer. I watched in amazement. Dewey fired a convertible at the printer. *Smack!* Zachary's hand shot out to slap it away. He stopped a fire engine with his chest. He deflected an ambulance with a high-flailing sneaker. *Nothing* got by him!

"Come on, Adam," he panted. "Grab him!"

But I was really enjoying the acrobatic display. "Nice save!" I cheered. I realized it *was* a save, just like a hockey goalie's. Only I'd like to see Brendan do *that*. Heck, I'd be interested to see if his brother Tony could pull off some of Zachary's moves!

Then I caught sight of an old pair of skates in the corner of the dweeb's closet and it hit me like four thousand pounds of wet cement. The Rangers needed a goalie. Man, our *own* goalie thought we needed a goalie! And here, before my very eyes, was the greatest natural stopper of all time.

Sure, he was untrained. He'd probably never strapped on pads in his life! But desperate times called for desperate measures. If we were going to have any chance at all against the Canadians, Zachary Gustafson — the Grand Poobah of the Loyal Order of Losers! — was going to stand in goal for the South Middle School Rangers! Unbelievable but true.

I grabbed his little brother to stop the attack. "Hey, Zack," I began. "Got any plans today?"

It took him a minute to catch his breath. "Well, I'll probably drop by the science fair and see how Milo's —" He stopped and looked at me in suspicion. "Why?"

The microdweeb started kicking at my ankles, but I ignored him. "How would you like to be a hero and fight for the honor of your school?"

Zachary made a face at me. "I'm not going to hold the chicken. She'll peck my eyes out."

"It's got nothing to do with the chicken," I insisted. "You're going to be the Rangers' new goalie!"

He couldn't have been more shocked if I'd told him he'd been elected homecoming queen. He just gawked at me, so I kept on going. "Yeah, I know you've never played before, but trust me, you're *awesome!* I watched you protecting your computer. You've got all the moves! It sounds crazy, but you can do this!"

He stared at me while all this sunk in. Then a slimy look took shape on his used-car-salesman features. "I'm banned from the rink, remember? Besides, what makes you think I want to help out your stupid hockey team? I don't recall you muscleheads going out of your way to be nice to me."

"That's ancient history," I said quickly. "Come on! And bring your skates —"

But Zachary wasn't finished. "I'm having a vision!" He closed his eyes like a fortune-teller. "Three words! Dweeb and geek and —"

"We were just joking —" I offered lamely.

"Loser!" He spat it out. "Wait, I'm having another memory —"

"Aw, come on —"

"Wedgies," Zachary said angrily. "I remember a lot of wedgies. Now get your hands off my brother, take your chicken, and beat it!"

There comes a point in every cool person's life when he has no choice but to get down on his knees and beg a dweeb. There was no question that this was my time. I took a deep breath and swallowed a smorgasbord of pride. I apologized for everything any Ranger had ever said or done to Zachary. Then I swore on the legends of Gordie Howe and Wayne Gretzky and all the hockey greats that no Ranger would ever so much as look funny at him — starting today until the end of time.

"Even if I stink," Zachary added, and I knew I'd won.

"You won't." I unhanded the baby and shouldered the spare equipment bag.

The Canadians game was a major tradition, so the Community Center was bustling. The arena was right across the foyer from the exhibition hall, so there was a huge traffic jam as hockey fans streamed around the science fair nerds, who were maneuvering bulky projects through the crowd into the fair.

Zachary tried to run into the exhibition hall. "Just let me talk to Milo."

"No time," I said, putting an iron grip on his dweeby shoulders.

"Hey, Milo!" he called into the busy hall, waving his arms. But I dragged him across the foyer and into our dressing room.

Coach Crenshaw was in the middle of a lecture about how he didn't want us to get spooked by playing without Henrietta. I rushed in and hoisted the spare equipment bag so the guys would know our mascot was there. A huge sigh of pure relief went up.

"Good," the coach approved. "I'm glad you guys have gotten over that crazy superstition. I want to hear everybody say it: 'The chicken doesn't skate.'"

"The chicken doesn't skate," we repeated.

"Squawk!"

The coach frowned, and I thought we were nailed for sure, when the team finally noticed Zachary. To say that he got a standing ovation would be a lie. The guys were ready to lynch him. *And* me for suggesting he might be our goalie.

"Are you nuts?"

"He cheered *against* us!"

"Get that creep out of here!"

"Come on, Lurie!" Coach Crenshaw added. "We did fine with our team the way it is! We're South Minnesota champions! We don't have to panic and make a bunch of crazy adjustments at the last minute!"

The babble of protest swelled up again, but Brendan quieted everybody down with a shrill, "Let's listen to what he has to say!"

Desperately, I collected my thoughts, searching for a way to convince everybody that this world-class loser should be a Ranger. "I know it's weird, but you've got to believe me! He could be the best goalie we've ever had! Better than Brendan — even better than Tony!"

The Wall?!" My teammates recoiled in amazement.

I looked from face to face. "I'm as loyal as anybody, but you all know we're going to get killed today. Give the dweeb — I mean Zachary — a chance."

"It's our only hope," Brendan added.

At first I thought Coach Crenshaw was going to put up an argument. Instead he just said, "Do it."

I started strapping Brendan's goalie pads onto Zachary's skinny legs.

"Aren't you going to tell them about our deal?" he whispered as I tightened the Velcro straps. "You know, no more wedgies?"

"Later," I muttered nervously.

If my teammates had been skeptical before, *now* they were on the point of revolution. Stupid Zachary could barely stand in all that goalie equipment. Once on the rink, he skated in tiny staccato steps, like a four-year-old who was just learning. When we put him in net for his warmup shots, he fell, bashing his face mask hard against the ice. We picked him up, dazed and wobbly, but he couldn't manage a goalie's crouch. Instead, he slumped, with his glove and stick arms hanging limp at his sides. He made no move to go after the easy practice shots the team slid by him.

"Lurie, have you gone crazy?" the coach rasped at me. "This kid's not a goalie! He can barely stand on his feet!"

I skated over to Zachary. "No, no, *no!*" I shouted. "Pretend the net is your computer and the puck is all that stuff your baby brother throws at it!"

The buzzer went off, signifying the start of the game. For me, it was like hearing the church bells of my own funeral.

"We need more time!" I pleaded to the ref, but he waved me into position for the national anthems.

I skated to the circle, feeling like my intestines had been hollowed out by piranhas. My deepest fear had just come true: In my crazed desire to have a chance against the Canadians, I had destroyed my own team.

23

FROM THE CLIPBOARD OF COACH CRENSHAW

I knew we didn't stand a chance against the Canadians. We *never* have! Oh, sure, back when I was a kid we squeaked by them once. But what nobody remembers was that there was a teachers' strike in Winnipeg that year, so they had to send us a team from this little farm school outside the city. Maybe that was why I was desperate enough to put Gustafson in goal. Besides, everyone knew Lurie would saw both his legs off before he'd hurt the team.

Or so I'd thought. Gustafson wasn't a goalie! He could barely stand on his skates! That's when the extent of my blunder came crashing down on me.

"Walters!" I bawled. "Get some pads on!"

"But Coach," he protested. "Zachary's got my jersey."

"I don't care if you play *naked!*" I growled. "Hurry!"

The players were livid. All through both national anthems: "He stinks, Coach!" "He can't even skate!" "Why's he in there, Coach?"

"*Squawk!*"

I froze. "What was that?"

A few "What was that?"'s bubbled around the bench. I looked around. Between the music and the nervous buzz of the crowd, maybe I was hearing things. The arena practically vibrated with anticipation.

Come on Walters!

But he didn't make it before the anthems ended. We were going to have to play the first couple of shifts with Gustafson.

The referee dropped the puck. The Rebels' captain won the draw and ploughed over Lurie like he was a speed bump.

"Hit him!" I cried.

The kid made a beautiful deke, and Tenorio missed his check. The captain streaked in, raised his stick, and fired a blistering shot.

Gustafson didn't move. At first, I thought he didn't even see the puck hurtling for the top corner of the net. Then, almost like a mechanical response, his glove arm snapped up and grabbed the puck out of the air.

"*What a save!*" bellowed a voice, and I realized in shock that it was mine.

Lurie picked himself up off the ice and rushed our goalie, joyously crying "Za-a-ack!"

The face-off moved to our end. Gustafson made an impossible stick save, knocked away a sure goal with his blocker, and pounced on a dangerous rebound.

"Did you see that?" Sorrentino was bug-eyed. "He froze the puck right off their captain's stick!"

"He's not human!" breathed Walters, who was dressed to play but thrilled that he wasn't needed.

"I always knew he wasn't human," grumbled Hughes. "I just never realized he was a goalie."

"Hey!" came Ginsberg's righteous voice from the seats above our bench. "Just because Zachary isn't one of the 'beautiful people,' doesn't mean he can't be a good player!"

I turned to face her. "I thought you only cared about the chicken. Why are you here *now?*"

"Are you kidding?" she cried, a little too loudly. "I'm a Ranger fan! Go team go!"

"Squawk!"

I turned to face my team. "Guys, what's going on?"

A roar from the crowd snapped my attention back to the game. I looked to the ice just in time to see Gustafson snatch a booming shot right out of the air. I couldn't believe this was the same kid who couldn't do a single chin-up and refused to climb the ropes in gym because of his fear of heights.

He was putting on a superstar performance. The

Rebels were all over us. The shots-on-goal counter showed 23–2, but the kid stopped everything. The first period ended with the score 0–0.

I couldn't resist. In the locker room I lifted Gustafson up, equipment and all, and enfolded him in a big bear hug. "You're amazing!"

His reply was to the team, not me: "This means no more wedgies, right? Adam said."

I couldn't let it go. "Where did you learn to play like that?"

He shrugged. "It's pretty easy. I mean, there's only one puck out there. Doomsday can throw things five or six at a time."

"*Squawk!*"

This time I wasn't hearing things. There was no game noise, no roar of the crowd. Only one thing on earth could warble like that, and it wasn't the Zamboni.

"All right," I demanded, "where is she?"

Dead silence. "No girls in the locker room, Coach," Lurie said finally.

I glared at him. "Milo Neal's chicken is in this room. I heard her!"

"Maybe you heard, like, some *other* chicken," Hughes suggested.

"A stray," Sorrentino added hopefully.

"Maybe the building is infested." *That* was Vincent.

"With *chickens*?!" I exploded. "Look, guys, I understand, okay? She's a great mascot. I'm a Ranger, too. But

I have to be a teacher first! That bird is stolen merchandise! Holding her is a *crime!* I can't have that on my team, and neither can you!"

But the guys stonewalled me. I searched all the lockers, the shower stalls, and the laundry bin.

"Squawk!"

"Oh, come on!" I shouted in frustration. It was a chicken, not a microdot! How could they possibly keep it hidden?

The buzzer sounded and the crowd cheered us back to the ice. When Gustafson came over the boards, the noise level went through the roof. He got a standing ovation.

I tried to concentrate on the game. Really, I did. But I just couldn't get that fugitive chicken out of my head. We went on the power play; I thought about Henrietta. A questionable off-side call; I scanned the bench, looking for hiding places. There was a scramble in front of the net — *missing chicken.* Gustafson was flat on his back — *Henrietta* — under at least two Rebels. The puck went to this huge kid, who flipped it — *kidnapped chicken* — right at the net. Out of nowhere, a glove reached out of the pile of people and caught it. *Where was that stupid chicken?!*

"Great shift, guys!" cheered Tenorio as the exhausted skaters climbed over the boards.

"Did you see that?" gasped Lurie. "Zack picked one right out of the top corner!" He threw off his helmet, wrapped his head in a large towel, and bent over the spare equipment bag, catching his breath.

"Careful!" I barked when I saw the towel dangling to the floor off the bench. "You're going to trip somebody with that!"

"Sorry, Coach." Lurie stood up.

A second later, when I glanced down the bench, it was Sorrentino crouched under the towel. The next time I looked, there was Tenorio in the same pose. Were my players really *so* exhausted? I squinted at Tenorio doubled over the spare equipment bag. Tenorio wasn't gasping. He'd been off the ice for a while. What was he — what were all of them doing under that towel?

Ohhhhhhh . . .

Suddenly I knew how detectives must feel when they crack the big case. It all came to me — the towel wasn't for drying; it was for hiding. Hiding the duffel. And what could be in the duffel? You didn't have to be a rocket scientist to figure it out.

I saw that Lurie had noticed my interest. "Adam," I said softly, "hand over the bag."

He looked at me beseechingly. "Coach, you can't. Not now."

"The chicken doesn't skate," I reminded him.

"Yeah, I know, but maybe she *sort of* does. You know?"

The weird thing was, I *did* know. I hesitated. I could lose my job if I didn't deliver the chicken to Mr. Delong right away. But these were the *Canadians*! And thanks to Gustafson, we had a chance. Heck, at this point in the Canadians game we were usually down by five or six goals. Call me crazy, I reached for the duffel.

"The bag," I ordered.

Lurie was in agony. "Coach — *please!*"

I looked him in the eye. "I need to count the backup elbow pads," I said stiffly.

The kid stared at me for a moment, and then a slow smile took shape behind his breath-fogged visor. "Yes, sir, Coach!" He placed the duffel on the floor in front of me. The whole team gathered around breathlessly.

As I bent down and unzipped the bag, Sorrentino draped the towel over my head. Sure enough, that goofy chicken head bobbed up at me. "Hello, uh, Henrietta," I began. How do you talk to a chicken? "Milo says you're a brainless bag of oven stuffer, and now's the time to prove him wrong," I said, hoping my wife never found out about this. "So how about a goal —"

That's when I heard Lurie yelling, "DeeVee! *No!*"

I snapped up just in time to see Vincent at the Rebels' blue line. His face was bright red, a study in pure concentration; his stick was raised back so far it was pointing straight up at the heavens.

"Vincent!" I bellowed. "Not a slap shot! Not *now!* I'll bench you for the rest of your life!"

POW!!! He hit the puck with the force of a meteor

slamming into a mountain. The enormous effort landed the kid flat on the ice.

"No!" I shouted. But I could see right away that there was something different about this slap shot. Instead of taking off for Jupiter, it stayed low. The puck sizzled in like a cruise missile, about three inches off the ice. It streaked past the defensemen, shot past the goalie, ripped clear through the mesh of the back of the net, and split the boards with a mighty *crack!* The red goal light flashed on.

The crowd erupted with a deafening roar. My players cleared the bench and I'm not embarrassed to say, so did I. Vincent was just getting back to his feet, but we knocked him down again and piled on, howling with joy. I have to admit I was as bad as any of the kids.

Vincent looked up me. "I'm sorry, Coach. I had to take it —"

Lurie cut him off, laughing with glee. "DeeVee, you big dope, you *scored!*"

Vincent sat up and stared at the puck, which was still wedged in the boards behind the torn net. "*I* scored?" he barely whispered.

"Yeah!" It came from everybody.

"With my slap shot?"

"Yeah!" I could see the emotion twist that crazy kid's face — I knew he was thinking about the countless hours of firing tennis balls against his garage door, the

arguments with me and his teammates over that con-
founded slap shot, the games spent riding the pine because of it. He might never score again, but this was
Donald Vincent's moment. He burst into tears.

It was the most touching scene in all my years of
coaching. Vincent bawling uncontrollably, Lurie trying
to dry the kid's tears through the visor, the others slapping Vincent's helmet and shoulder pads, the roaring
crowd, thunder in our ears. Right then I knew why I became a coach.

"All right, break it up!" The officials began pulling
us apart. When the referee saw me he gawked. "Crenshaw, what are you doing out here?" Then he spotted
Vincent's tear-streaked face. "Injured player?"

I grinned. "More like a lifelong dream fulfilled."

He looked at me in disgust. "You're supposed to be
keeping them in line, not egging them on!"

When I got up, I caught sight of Mr. Delong watching
disapprovingly from the bleachers. But at that moment,
I wasn't a teacher; I was a *Ranger!*

"Number one!" I bellowed, and my players gave me
a cheering escort to the bench.

In the stands, Mr. Delong shook his head at me. I
didn't care. We were destined for greatness today. I
could feel it in my bones!

24

DOWNLOADED FROM THE FILES OF ZACHARY GUSTAFSON

If you live long enough, you become what you despise the most. In my case, that happened when I became a member of the South Middle School Rangers. Worse, I was the star.

That might explain why the crowd had been chanting *"Zack Attack! Zack Attack!"* ever since the start of the third period. They went totally gaga every time I touched the puck. It was more than a little weird to be suddenly awesome at something you didn't even like — almost like getting elected president when you weren't running. But to be honest, this goalie gig was not such a big deal! Compared to the barrage my brother, Doomsday, fired at my computer, the Rebels were nothing special.

They were a lot better than us, of course. That was pretty obvious. I was making saves four, five, even six at a time before my defensemen could clear the zone. When I wasn't flopping around stopping pucks, I checked out the shots-on-goal counter. 51–2 . . . 64–3 . . . 72–4 . . . was this even fair? I looked over at the Rebels' goalie. He was enjoying peace and solitude. Me? I was Mr. Bull's-eye in a shooting gallery. Which gave me a thought for a new screenplay: *A warrior tribe on a distant planet. Every year, a young brave is selected for target practice for the flaming poison acid-dipped flesh-goring arrow archers. Then this race of mutant highly intelligent chickens* — a booming slap shot bounced off my goalie mask with the force of a battering ram. I had to be on my toes to pounce on the rebound.

Lafayette hauled me to my feet and slapped me on the back. "Way to go, Zack!"

"Great save, buddy!" cheered Steve.

That was another weird thing about today. All those guys who picked on me and gave me wedgies — all of a sudden they *loved* me! They *pampered* me! And boy, did I rub their faces in it! I sent them to the bench for towels. I made them clean the snow off my skate blades. I was constantly getting my stick retaped. I asked for Gatorade at almost every whistle. Not because I wanted it, but because I couldn't resist the sight of those big hockey muscleheads breaking their necks to cater to my every whim.

This was a big mistake, which became obvious as the clock ticked down to the final minutes. Hockey games didn't have bathroom breaks, and I'd polished off about four bottles of Gatorade!

By the four-minute mark, it was a noticeable pressure. Within sixty seconds, I was grimacing behind my mask. Remember — you can't cross your legs when you're wearing goalie pads. When the clock stopped with 1:58 still to play, I felt like my back teeth were floating. A single thought dominated my brain: *I'm not going to make it!*

"Time out!" I headed off the ice, not so much skating as running on the toes of my skate blades.

"We've *used* our time-out!" Adam yelled at me.

"Gustafson, get back here!" That was Coach Crenshaw. I heard him just as I leaped off the ice and hurled myself into the rest room. I was going to catch a lot of flak over this, but I wasn't making my own decisions at that point. The Gatorade was definitely in charge.

Have you ever gone to the bathroom in full goalie equipment? It's like dismantling a car engine. Ninety percent of that stuff has to come off. It's a major operation! By the time I got back to the ice, both teams were standing around waiting, the refs were glaring at me, and Coach Crenshaw's eyes looked like they were about to pop out of his head.

"That's a *double* delay-of-game penalty!" the referee

roared in my face. "One for calling a time-out you don't have, and one for *taking* it!"

"That's-not-right-a-two-man-advantage-it's-like-giving-them-a-sure-goal-we-don't-stand-a-chance-why-don't-you-just-hand-them-the-game-on-a-silver-platter-it's-not-fair!" Coach Crenshaw, Adam, and I all screamed it out so fast, it was impossible to tell who said what. But referees are like the weather — they don't change no matter how much you complain.

"Aw, Zack!" Adam seethed.

It looked pretty grim. I mean, the Canadians had nearly eighty shots at me *at even strength*! With two extra players, it was going to be open season on Zachary, and all the hunters had bazookas. Then the Rebels pulled their goalie for an extra skater. That meant they'd have six attackers — against only three defenders and, gulp, me.

It was total chaos — like a hundred Deweys, all throwing blocks at the same time. My three teammates — Adam, Joey, and Steve — formed a triangle to protect the net. But they were trying to stop up Niagara Falls with a cotton ball. Four-inch armor plating wouldn't have protected the net from the offensive barrage the Rebels unleashed at me.

It was all happening too fast to think about what was going on. My mind shut down and a kind of weird automatic pilot took over. My catching glove was just a blur; my blocker and stick worked in perfect unison; my legs were everywhere; hard shots slamming into the goalie pads resounded like drums. Slap shot! *Stick save!* Backhand! *Off the chest!* Wrist shot! *What a catch!* Scramble in front of the net! I dove on the puck. How did I know what to do? No idea! Hey, I'd only been a goalie for an hour or so. The shots-on-goal counter showed 89–4. And through it all the crowd chanted, *"Zack Attack! Zack Attack!"*

Fourteen seconds to play. I huddled with Adam, Joey, and Steve, but we were gasping and choking too much to say anything. Actually, words weren't necessary. The situation was obvious — even to a non-hockey fan like me: If we held out against the on-slaught, we'd beat the Canadians for the first time in thirty-five years. If we let them tie it up, we were probably going to get creamed in overtime.

Fourteen seconds. What was fourteen seconds? A lifetime, that's what. It stood between me and no more wedgies. Respect at school. Power, even. Why, as a hockey hero, they'd owe me big.

The puck was dropped. The Rebels' captain won the draw and passed back to his defenseman.

Pow! A booming slap shot was headed for the net. But with all the traffic in front of me, I couldn't see a thing! Then, at the last instant, I caught a hint of black. Desperately, I went into a full split, kicking out my leg. The puck caromed off the toe of my skate.

"Rebound!" shouted Joey.

The puck was just sitting there, fat and inviting. I hurled myself at it, but the Rebels' captain had the same idea. *Crunch!* I bounced off that sasquatch like a Ping-Pong ball, and careened right into Adam. The two of us landed in a heap behind the net.

No one was yelling "Zack Attack" now. They were just yelling.

The wheels of time seemed to grind to a halt to give me a chance to savor the exquisite agony of the moment: There were two seconds left on the clock. The Rebels' captain had the puck right in front of a totally empty net. His wrists twitched as he prepared to pop in the tying goal.

"No-o-o-o-o!!" screamed Adam beside me.

Suddenly he grabbed me by the suspenders of my hockey pants — one final giant wedgie to end all wedgies! He lifted me up, up, and over the top of the net. And as I came down in a perfect swan dive, I swung my goalie stick at the puck.

Thwack! What a beautiful sound. I hit the puck about a trillionth of an inch before it crossed the goal line. And just as I landed face-first on the ice, the buzzer sounded to end the game. Final score 1–0 Rangers. *Miracle.*

The Community Center seated fifteen hundred people. And when they all leaped to their feet at the same time, it almost created a wind. The roar of celebration was that much louder because it was thirty-seven years

in coming. My teammates — those rotten Rangers, those
muscleheads who made a career out of bugging me —
they lifted me up on their shoulders and carried me
around the ice for a victory lap.

"Remember," I shouted down at them, spelling out
the deal, "no more wedgies!"

But you couldn't talk to people who were screaming
with joy. Adam's face was so pink that if you put lace
around it, it would have been a valentine! This was
probably the greatest moment in the guy's life! And
there was DeeVee — still crying! Coach Crenshaw was
kissing guys on the helmet! It was disgusting! Lynette
leaped the boards and threw herself into Joey's arms. So
I guess the on-again off-again was on again. And all this
happiness was because of me! I was underwhelmed.

Lynette was the first pebble of the avalanche. They
started coming over the boards like army ants, howling
and cheering. Pretty soon you couldn't see the ice for
the swarms of people. It was like New Year's Eve —
everywhere you looked it was a party — friends dancing and singing, proud parents hugging their sons,
teachers congratulating the coach, a chicken darting
through the forest of skates and legs —

A *chicken?!*

I screamed, *"Henrietta's loose!"*

Ploughing through the crowd like a harvester through
a field of wheat came Kelly Marie. "Where? *Where?
WHERE?!"*

From my perch atop everybody's shoulders, I pointed. Henrietta was scrambling and skittering her way across the rink. A buzz of recognition shot through the crowd.

"Is that a chicken?"

"It's the Neal kid's chicken!"

"The *missing* chicken!"

"Grab her!"

"*No!*" screamed Kelly Marie. "You'll hurt her!"

Mr. Lurie snatched up the bird, but Henrietta flapped wildly and broke free. Everyone made a try for that slippery chicken, *including* the team, so I got dumped on my face. I wasn't the only one. People were diving for Henrietta, slipping on the ice and knocking each other over. If I ever switched my screenwriting style over to comedy, I'd have tons of ideas for my first movie, called *Henrietta vs. The Fifteen Hundred Stooges.*

Out of the sea of grabbing, diving, falling players and spectators rose Henrietta, flapping her wings furiously. She got just enough lift to land her on top of the boards. Then she jumped down and scooted out of the arena.

"*She's getting away!*" shrieked Kelly Marie.

I was the first one over the boards and hot on her tail feathers. Running on skates in full goalie equipment was no easy matter. But I could feel fifteen hundred people swarming behind me. If I stopped, I'd be trampled by the thundering herd. So I chased the bird across the foyer, my skate blades making hideous grinding sounds on the terrazzo floor. With a sinking heart, I realized that Henrietta was heading straight into the exhibition hall and — oh, no! — the science fair!

"Don't go in there!" I shouted. Like she was going to listen! Talk about the worst thing that could possibly happen! That science fair was scheduled to be her funeral! She was supposed to be there not as a guest but as *lunch*! If it came out that I was one of the kidnappers, Milo would never speak to me again. Not to mention that Adam, Kelly Marie, and I would probably get suspended and maybe even arrested as cattle rustlers.

Science fairs were definitely not designed for a hockey team on skates. I stopped short to avoid plowing into display tables and experiments, and everyone else piled up behind me, gridlocked in the doorway. I dropped to my knees and crawled after Henrietta under the tables. Hopping and hustling, the bird led me on a merry chase *beneath* the science fair, navigating through a maze of table legs. For once, I was grateful for my equipment, which was saving me a lot of scrapes, bangs, and bruises. I hadn't crawled this much since I was Doomsday's age. It was murder! I didn't get to stand up until Henrietta emerged from under the experiment tables.

I rolled out into the aisle, leaped to my feet — and found myself staring into the world-famous face of

Victor Neal! I was awestruck. The real California famous guy! He looked exactly like on TV — better even, because we didn't get the Science Channel, so I usually saw him scrambled.

I was so profoundly shocked that it took a second for me to realize I was standing right in front of "The Complete Life Cycle of a Link in the Food Chain." Milo and Mrs. Baggio were opposite me, offering a bucket of fried chicken to two men wearing JUDGE badges.

"Zachary?" Milo blurted, squinting into my face through the bars of my goalie mask. But he was distracted by a loud squawk. There was a mad flurry of white feathers and Henrietta, the lost specimen, flapped her way straight up Milo's chinos and into his arms.

Milo's eyes bulged behind his Bertrand St. Renes. "Where did she come from?"

Victor Neal laughed. "What do you care so long as she's here? Talk about timing!"

Milo turned urgently to the judges. "Would it be possible for my project to be judged last? That would give me about an hour."

The men exchanged shrugs. "Sounds fair enough if there's a good reason," said the senior of the two.

"I'm taking the specimen to Arno's Butcher Shop," Milo explained. "I should have just enough time to cook the meat and we can truly complete the link in the food chain."

Victor Neal snapped to attention. "Milo, what do you mean? You're not still planning to kill that bird?!"

Milo looked confused. "Of course I am. The experiment —"

"Milo, *think!*" his father cut him off. "You've been around that chicken for four months now! It's not a specimen anymore — it's a *friend!*"

"Dad!" Milo couldn't believe his ears. "You of all people should know that a chicken doesn't have the necessary intelligence to be capable of friendship! It's — it's *bad science!*"

"Bad science," retorted Victor Neal, "is ignoring what's right in front of your nose! That chicken got frightened in the crowd and came running right to you! She *knows* you! And you want to eat her? Have a heart!"

Milo flinched as if he'd just been slapped. The poor kid was destroyed. All he ever wanted was to live up to his dad in science, and here was that same dad, wailing out on him! That was when I said my first words ever to the great Victor Neal. But they weren't, "Hi, I'm Milo's best friend in the world," or, "Hey, I understand you hang out with lots of Hollywood bigwig types," or even, "Wait here while I go get the fifty pounds of movie scripts in the steamer trunk in my closet." I didn't say any of that stuff.

Instead, I turned on the great man and barked, "Wait

a minute! Milo's worked like a dog on this project to make you proud! You don't even visit him for four months, and now you show up just to *yell* at the guy?"

What have I done?! My blunder stretched in all directions to infinity. I had been praying, hinting, *scheming* to finagle a meeting with this man ever since I first laid eyes on Milo. And what did I do with this golden opportunity? I chewed out this Nobel Prize scientist in public in his own hometown. Good-bye Hollywood.

Victor Neal was giving me the worm guts look — at least now I knew where Milo got it. His expression would have put out a forest fire.

Timidly, Milo said, "Dad, I don't think you've met my friend Zach —" He fell silent, looking nervously down at Henrietta. She was making strange clucking noises and wriggling around in his arms. I'd been scratched and pecked more than anybody, but I'd never seen her like this before.

"Maybe she's just frightened by all the people," offered Mrs. Baggio. "Hold her tight."

Then the bird started cackling and shaking. Milo's eyes filled with wonder. He said, "Oh . . . oh . . . oh, wow . . ."

He reached under Henrietta and pulled out a gleaming white egg.

Victor Neal snapped his fingers. "That's it! There's your food chain, Milo!"

"You're right!" Excitedly, Milo turned to the judges. "It still counts, doesn't it? The chicken was raised, consumed food, and eventually *produced* food."

"It's even better," Mrs. Baggio added breathlessly. "Henrietta will provide eggs for a long time."

The senior judge threw his head back and laughed. "You're a lucky kid, Milo Neal!" he exclaimed. "It happened at the last second, but your link in the food chain is complete!"

"FREEZE!!"

The crowd parted to admit Kelly Marie, approaching like a gunslinger. Only instead of a six-shooter she had the exhibition hall fire extinguisher with the nozzle pointed at Milo. I was fascinated. It was a true screenwriting moment — the standoff. All the best movies have them. You don't get a lot of standoffs in St. Martin, Minnesota. I waited, not even breathing.

She addressed our teacher first. "I'm sorry, Mrs. Baggio."

"But Kelly Marie —" exclaimed Milo.

"Quiet!" she thundered. "Now hand over that chicken! And no sudden movements!"

"Now, just one moment, young lady!" Victor Neal stepped out in front of his son.

Kelly Marie panicked. She yanked the pin and a mountain of foam exploded out of the nozzle right onto Professor Neal. It all happened in the blink of an eye.

One second Milo's father was standing there. The next, he was a statue of white fluffy suds.

"Dad!" cried Milo.

"Don't shoot!" ordered Mrs. Baggio, which was kind of like shutting the barn door after the horse was already long gone.

"Henrietta's fine," I told Kelly Marie. "She just laid an egg. *That's* the food chain they're talking about. You just slimed Victor Neal!"

"Really?" Ever the quick-change artist, Kelly Marie enfolded her victim in a big hug. "I knew you'd come when you got my letter!"

"Miss Ginsberg, I presume," said Milo's dad, spitting foam.

Sheepishly, Kelly Marie used the sleeve of her sweatshirt to wipe the suds from the famous face. The crowd of hockey players and spectators who had been filing into the hall recognized Victor Neal and burst into applause.

The astronomer put an arm around his son's shoulders, sharing some of the foam. "I'm sorry, Milo. Really I am. I should have come sooner, but you know my schedule —"

"It's okay, Dad."

"No, it's not," his father persisted. "Your friend Zeke is right —"

"That's Zachary," I chimed in. "Have you ever met Steven Spielberg?"

I wasn't even miffed that they both ignored me. Great screenplays have heartwarming moments, too, and this was one of them. Arm in arm, father and son walked off to get reacquainted. It would have been a five-hanky moment if one of the characters wasn't covered from head to toe in fire extinguisher foam.

Fade to black . . .

25

DOWNLOADED FROM THE FILES
OF ZACK·MASTER GOAL·STOP·SON

HENRIETTA: CHICKEN OF VALOR

[Scene 48]

[INTERIOR: Science Fair – day]

Could this be the end of Henrietta? The HOCKEY
PLAYERS cry into their face guards as the oil in the
electric wok heats up and begins to sizzle, a stir-fried
grave for a beloved friend.

[CLOSE-UP: MR. ARNO, sharpening his cleaver.]

VICTOR NEAL

There's a way, son. There's always a way. Don't lose
hope. Be brave like this valiant chicken, and look within

yourself for the solution that will let Henrietta live to cluck another day!

HENRIETTA

Squawk!

MILO

(bravely)

Oh, yes, Dad!

> [VIEW ON HENRIETTA: An egg comes out of wherever eggs come out of on a chicken.]

I sat back from my computer. That last part wasn't very professional. Oh, well, I'd ask Milo where the eggs come from when he and Henrietta got back from the state science fair in Duluth. With the chicken laying an egg every day, he must have been a pretty big expert by now.

Things were pretty dull with Henrietta in Duluth. Mr. Delong officially declared her the school mascot for all teams and she was going to live in the pen in Mrs. Baggio's room. Why waste a perfectly good chicken coop? In theory, the bird belonged to all of us equally. But in reality she was Kelly Marie's sweetie. Oh, sure, the usual band of chicken wackos were still hanging around — Joey and Lynette, Sheila and Brendan. Even Milo called her "Henrietta" now, instead of "the specimen." *I* was the only one she hated, and I had a giant scratch on my nose to prove it.

The excitement of the big game was pretty much over by now. Yet every once in a while, some goofball would say, "Hey, we beat the Canadians!" and bang, it was celebration time all over again. Frankly, I was getting a little sick of all that yahooing.

But I shouldn't complain. That hockey game changed life a lot for me. I was now on the guest list for all of Lynette's parties. As co-MVPs, DeeVee and I got to share the hammock. Third-graders asked for my autograph on the street. High school guys *talked* to me. I wasn't a dweeb anymore. I was Zack-master Goal-stop-son, the Zack Attack, the Super-Wall.

Adam pestered me twenty-four hours a day. "Aw, come on, Zack! You've got to join the team. With me in eighth grade, you in net, and Henrietta on the bench, we'll be *awesome!* We'll go undefeated and *destroy* the Canadians!"

"Well, I'm not really sure. I'm pretty busy with my writing." Oh, I'd probably do it, but I got a major kick out of stringing the guy along. I didn't intend to sign up for hockey until five minutes before the opening face-off next October. Let him sweat; let them all sweat. Payback for a lifetime of wedgies.

"Please, Zack! It's my last year! I won't sleep till I know you're on the team!" The musclehead even tried to get me to take French with him next semester. Want to hear the logic? So when we were in the NHL together, we could give interviews *en français* in Montreal. Well, okay, maybe my goalie talent is headed for the NHL — but I'd better get drafted by the L.A. Kings. Because there's no way I'm going to let hockey stardom interfere with my screenwriting career!

South Middle School gave Milo a hero's welcome when he and Henrietta won the state science fair. It was Mrs. Baggio's first state winner ever. Kelly Marie, of course, gave all the credit to the chicken. I could see Milo didn't care so much about the trophy. He was thrilled that he'd get to go to the national finals and be with his dad.

I went over to help him pack and say bon voyage. Kelly Marie was already there, trying to convince him that Henrietta had to fly first class. You should have seen her face when she found out her sweetie was going in a box in the baggage compartment.

While Milo was showing her out, I took the opportunity to stick a few of my screenplays into his suitcase — you know, the really classy ones like *Terror in the Sewer*, *Horrordome*, and, of course, *The Brain Eaters*. If things got dull, maybe Professor Neal would need something to read. I'd be friends with Milo no matter what; but it seemed stupid to pass up a perfectly good Hollywood connection.

It paid off, too. Victor Neal got hold of *Terror in the Sewer* and actually gave it to a friend who worked at Paramount. Mom almost blew a gasket when I got a letter on real studio stationery. I mean, she was just now getting used to me being a sports hero.

The Paramount guy wasn't that smart because he rejected *Terror in the Sewer*. But he encouraged me to keep writing. He also suggested that I tone down the blood and guts and death, and try to concentrate more on my own experience.

So here I was, hard at work on *Henrietta: Chicken of Valor*, telling the story of the last few months . . .

MILO

(holding up the egg)

This chicken has taught us all a valuable lesson . . .

(organ music swells)

. . . that you should never give up! That it's always darkest before the dawn! And that it takes a brave heart to be a chicken!

> He is interrupted by the ringing of VICTOR NEAL's cellular phone.

VICTOR NEAL

(flipping open the phone)

Neal here . . .

VOICE ON PHONE

It's no use, Vic! The planetary high-magnification Cosmo-scope has detected a giant asteroid hurtling toward the earth!

[EXTERIOR: Outer space]

The out-of-control planetoid streaks past the rings of Saturn, narrowly misses the moons of Jupiter, rips the atmosphere away from Mars, and plows right into Earth.

KA-BOOM!!! Our planet is vaporized in a humongous celestial fireworks display. Five billion perish, not including animals and plants. It is the end of all life as we know it.

ROLL CLOSING CREDITS

Okay, I know it didn't happen exactly that way. Like, Victor Neal might have had a cell phone, but it didn't ring. And all that stuff about the earth getting destroyed, obviously.

Like it or lump it, that's my style.

Fade to black . . .

GORDON KORMAN was inspired to write *The Chicken Doesn't Skate* during a school visit in Michigan, where a middle-school class really did study "The Complete Life Cycle of a Link in the Food Chain." By the end of the experiment, the students were as attached to their chicken as the students in this book were!

Gordon Korman has written more than twenty books for middle-grade and young-adult readers, among them: *Why Did the Underwear Cross the Road?*, *The Toilet Paper Tigers*, and seven books in the popular *Bruno and Boots* series—all published by Scholastic. He divides his time between New York City, Pompano Beach, Florida, and Toronto, Canada, where he has been playing hockey since the age of seven.

Turn the page for an exciting **Q&A** with

Gordon Korman!

Q: What inspired you to write *The Chicken Doesn't Skate*? Which part or idea came to you first?

A: *The Chicken Doesn't Skate* is one of my only books that is based on a true story—not the hockey part, but the chicken plotline. I did an author visit at a middle school where they actually did Milo's project—raising a baby chick to adulthood in class with the intention of killing, cooking, and eating it once it was a full-grown hen. But by that time, the entire class had adopted the bird as the class pet, and there was a huge uproar over taking it to the butcher shop.

Q: Is hockey your favorite sport?

A: I grew up in Canada, so hockey was a central part of my childhood. We're pretty much born with hockey sticks in our cradles. I played from about first grade through the end of high school.

Q: Have you ever had a mascot that meant a lot to you as a hockey player?

A: I never became obsessed with a mascot, but it is true that hockey players are spectacularly superstitious. That's where the title comes from. When the players are convinced that they can't win without Henrietta, the poor coach just about loses his mind: *The chicken doesn't take slap shots! The chicken doesn't score goals! The chicken doesn't even skate!*

Q: *The Chicken Doesn't Skate* brings together a bunch of unlikely characters—a hockey team captain, a science nerd, a screenwriter, a class psychologist, and a chicken. Which one do you most identify with? Which one do you most aspire to or like the best?

A: I love to tell a story from multiple perspectives because I love how the same events can seem totally different when seen through different eyes. My favorite character was Zachary—the screenwriter—because he's so awful, yet, deep down, you know he's a good guy. I think we all have friends like Zachary.

Q: What was the worst science experiment you've had to do?

A: My high school science lab had a "ripple tank" to study wave behavior, and someone added soap to the water, so I ended up covered in suds.

Q: Did you know how the many storylines would come together at the end of the story when you started writing? Or did you have trouble deciding which side should win and how?

A: I'm a pretty big planner, because I find it makes the writing process so much easier. I knew exactly how the Henrietta/science project plot would turn out. The hockey storyline was a little more up in the air, but I was certain that I wanted an unexpected twist at the end. I write the kind of books that invite a lot of predictions, so I like to keep my readers guessing.

Q: What do you find is the most difficult part about writing a book?

A: I have the most trouble with the transition between beginning and middle.

Q: What's the easiest part about writing a book for you?

A: Because I'm such a plotter, endings are where I feel the most in control, since that's where everything comes together.

Q: Your books tend to be very action and adventure, or completely hilarious. Do you find one style easier or more fun to write?

A: Right now, I love switching back between a variety of styles—humor, adventure, sports, historical fiction, and then there's the series The 39 Clues, where I'm part of a team of authors. For a writer, the real enemy is boredom. If you're bored writing, you write boring.

Q: Is it harder to write humor for middle grade readers, or for teens?

A: Obviously, when you're writing for a very young audience, all you have to do is mention underwear, and you'll get laughs. But as your readers get older, the humor has to be more subtle. Also, with a younger crew, simply being funny can function as an end in itself, whereas in the teen world, the humor has to be an organic part of the greater whole.

Q: What's your writing process like? Do you start with an outline?

A: I'm a big outline guy. I need the beginning, the ending, and a couple of events from the middle before I start writing. Then, as the first draft progresses, more and more details fall into place. By the time I reach the ending, I pretty much know how it should go beat by beat.

Q: Do you prefer the very first draft, with a blank page or computer screen, or do you look forward to revisions? Or going on tour?

A: There's an immense feeling of satisfaction to finishing a new novel. But I do love going on tour and meeting my readers. I continue to do dozens of school visits every year.

Q: What does a day in the life of Gordon Korman look like? What's changed from when *The Chicken Doesn't Skate* was first published in 1996?

A: *The Chicken Doesn't Skate* was first published the year I got married. Now we have three kids, so my schedule centers around their schedules. I do most of my writing while they're at school—although I have to give them credit for letting me work when they're around.

Q: What's the strangest question you've ever gotten from a fan?

A: "Do you prefer discoing or waltzing?" Answer: Neither (I was a mosh-pit guy in my younger days).

Q: What's a question you've never been asked about your books or writing that you've always wanted to answer? (And, of course, what's the answer?)

A: "When are you going to write an important novel?" It's true that no one has ever finished one of my books and said, "Yep, now I know the meaning of life." But I do believe that my books are important, because they get kids psyched about reading. Sure, I don't have a mantle full of Newbery awards, but I have something even more important for a writer— fans, stretching all the way back to the release of my first book in 1978.

Q: Do you have any advice for young writers? What's the wackiest thing that works for your writing?

A: Ninety-five percent of what I know about writing comes from doing it, so my advice would be to keep on writing. It may not always be fun, but you will continue to get better. And I don't think this is all that wacky, but I am *nuts* about backing up my work. When I write something, I save it on my laptop, my desktop, and a flash drive. Then—just in case —I e-mail it to my cell phone *and* my parents' computer in Canada.

New York Times bestselling author
GORDON KORMAN
takes high jinks to new HEISTS!

When a mean collector swindles Griffin Bing out of a valuable Babe Ruth baseball card, he puts together a team of friends (and some enemies) to get it back. Griffin won't let his fortune go without a fight, even when his comic caper gets out of control.

When Griffin Bing's class visits a floating zoo, they don't expect to see animals being treated so badly. But as usual, Griffin has a plan— first rescue the animals, and then break them into a (better) zoo.